This is the inaugural issue of Underland Arcana, where the numinous, the esoteric, the supernatural, and the weird collide. It contains ghost stories, apocalyptic stories, stories about cats, stories about things that haunt the corner of your perception, stories hidden inside other stories, stories about cocktails and rivers and those last moments before everything goes black, and stories about the quiet fear that gets louder and louder and louder . . .

© 2021 Firebird Creative LLC and the respective contributors.

Underland Arcana is published quarterly. This issue is published in conjunction with the first new moon following the winter solstice.

EDITOR
Mark Teppo

COVER IMAGE
George Cotronis

SIGIL ART
Andrew Penn Romine

PUBLISHER
Underland Press
Clackamas, OR, USA

These stories are works of fiction. Names, characters, places, and incidents are the products of the author's imagination or are used in an absolutely fictitious manner. Any resemblance to actual events, locales, or persons—living or dead—is entirely coincidental.

All rights reserved, which means that no portion of this publication may be reproduced or transmitted, in any form or by any means, without the express written permission of the copyright holder(s).

These are the days . . .

www.underlandarcana.com

UNDERLAND ARCANA

~1~

Underland Press

Contents

The Draw

This is no secret: I love the tarot. The cards are a gateway to creative possibilities. Each deck reflects a different view of the Universe, even though the underlying symbology remains consistent (or not, which is another conversation for another time). While the cards are merely paint on paper, they unlock the amazing potential of our brains to ask "What if?"

Occassionally, I'll teach a class on jumpstarting a novel. We'll gather around and do a series of exercises that lead writers to something that waddles and quacks like an outline. Along the way, participants may find themselves stuck, and that's okay. I brought tarot cards. "If you don't know what happens next, ask for a card," I tell them. "And use it as a prompt."

Folks tend to laugh when I make this offer. They're sceptical of the magic I have in my hands. About halfway through the session, someone asks for a card. I provide it. At the next break, they confess it was exactly what they needed. And they ask how I knew which card to give them. I smile and shrug. The magician never shows their hand after all.

During the next portion, more writers ask for cards. The conversation expands. Some ask for a card—not because they need one, but because they are curious. What secret prompt do I offer? How do I always know to give them the card they really needed? I smile, shrug, and shuffle the deck for the next writer.

When I put out the call for stories, I said I did not want stories to be written to a specific card. "Hey, here's a Two of Wands story." "Oh, I've got a Ten of Cups fable for you." The magic would be in how the cards presented themselves later. Which, yes, to some degree, I'm interpreting these stories for you. But it's the Tarot, and so the *how?* and *why?* and *what if?* will be elusive.

Welcome to Underland Arcana.

Mark Teppo
January 12th, 2021

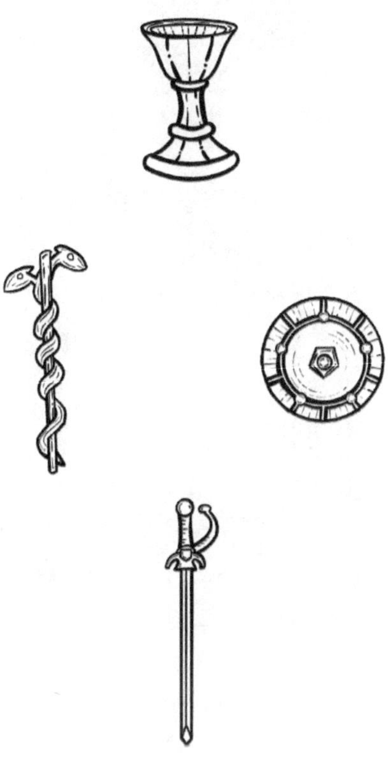

II

At the Heart of the River

~ *Jessie Kwak*

I have always loved you.

When you were a little boy, skipping stones across my broad back and plucking fat, splashing tadpoles from my shallows, I clung to you every time you left my banks. I was in the black dirt beneath your nails and the dank reek your mother would yell at you to wash off before dinner. Sometimes I would splash a daub of mud behind your ear and it would stay hidden there for days, weeks. Until you came back to me to play once again.

When you ran to me after your father came home drunk and vengeful, I saw you cry for the first time. The salt stung but I lapped your tears like they were the first fall rains when you heard him calling for you and sat up, stricken, splashing handfuls of me onto your face to hide your crying.

When you first brought *her*, I eddied and churned as you both slipped naked into me, tasting you both as you tasted each other. I decided quickly I didn't much care for her girlish giggle or the way she squealed in disgust when her toes squelched into the same black silk you'd smoothed over your boyish face as pretend camouflage years ago. I also didn't care for the bitter, toxic-tasting cologne you'd worn for her. I drew up icy currents from the deepest places in my heart until she shrieked, shivering, and begged you to go back to the shore. There, you drank cheap, sweet wine and made love for the first time on a blanket while I sulked and swept the bad taste farther downstream.

When you proposed, years later, you told her how much it meant to return to the place you first loved. She assumed where you first *made* love, but I knew the truth. *I* am the *place* you first loved. You tried to get down on a knee, but, no, it's too dirty, she said. She pulled you back up into her arms, but I seep into the soil, too, and I shifted beneath you both, just enough to make you lose your balance and step back with a yelp to splash your shoe into my shallows. You pulled her down with you and she caught her hand on a sharp rock. Her sun tan lotion smothered me in a greasy sheen, and the acrid metal you've put on her finger disgusted me. But I have a weakness for the taste of blood and I sucked at her hand greedily, pushed as much of myself into her wound as I could. You were laughing but she was angry, calling you clumsy, clutching her injured hand. Black silt and red blood dripped off her elbow into my lapping waves and I drank them both.

I have always loved you. And I still love you now, when you're fresh from her funeral in Sunday black. I'm sorry, my love. Although I won't lie and say I'm sad she's gone, you must believe me that this wasn't my intention. Infections simply have a way of spreading, and my silt is rich and alive.

I love you as you pick up rocks from my bank, examining them just as you did when you were a boy, looking for that perfectly shaped stone to skip across my back. I leap with joy that you might do so again—but, no. You're not looking for a smooth skipping stone, you're looking for a jagged one, like the one that tore her hand. Ah. I see.

You find one and cock your arm back to throw, and I will take your rocks hurled in anger just as happily as your rocks skipped in idle joy.

But you don't throw it.

You slip it into your pocket, instead; its jagged bulk juts against the fabric of your dress trousers. You pick up another stone, directly from my shallows, with no care this time for the stone's shape. Into your pocket it goes, a damp stain spreading out from your pocket.

You find another, another, reaching farther into my current, no heed paid to the state of your clothes or shoes as you wade in to fill your suit pockets with my stones. You fall to your knees and do not notice the pain, you bend back a fingernail and I taste blood; it's sweet, my love.

Now I'm too deep for you to crawl and you're walking, wading farther into me than you've ever gone, past the sun-warm swimming hole you built one teenaged summer and into the swift current at my heart.

Isn't it beautiful, the way the sunlight breaks the surface of the water and ripples in my currents? I lap kisses into your ears and nose, but your steps hesitate, hands clawing at your pockets.

Isn't it stunning, the way the schools of little silver minnows shatter like glass when you rush through, fingers pulling stones out of pockets to tumble downstream—I'll make them smooth, eventually.

Your mouth opens for breath and I fill you. Your arms windmill to swim and I dance with you, swirling us both as I've wanted to do all these years, tumbling us until you're dizzy.

Doesn't it move you, how lonely cold-cold-cold I am at my heart?

You seem tired of dancing, so I shift an ancient, slime-slick stone beneath your foot; your foot slips beneath and I hold you tight.

There's so much I've wanted to show you.

The Gardener

~ Michael Barsa

Behold the famous horror writer: pale, thin, disheveled, hunched over the greasy steering wheel and driving much too fast. His wife sits next to him. Usually she is the competent one, the one who drives, but not tonight. Tonight he has insisted. Snow whips through the headlight beams. The flakes are thick and frenzied, a snow globe shaken by a lunatic. He can just see where the road disappears around a bend. A ravine hugs the bend—a frown of ragged rock-teeth—and because they're in the country there is no barrier, only a skirt of gravel and a sign showing a truck tilting off a cliff.

His wife shifts in her seat, stirred from her usual boredom. "John," she says, training her huge gilt-framed sunglasses on him. Those sunglasses are like machinery, like a retractable roof, except they never retract: she wears them at all hours. Even so he can tell what she's thinking: that he's driving like this to prove a point. That he, as an author, believes he can do anything—defy the laws of gravity, of velocity and friction and the lubricity of ice. That he'd only have to utter the word *fly* and he could make it so.

She is right. But it is no game. The sign whips past. He makes a halfhearted attempt to turn the wheel.

They fly.

It takes him a moment to realize they've left the road, left solid ground itself. He feels it in his stomach first—a suspension, a disbelief. The engine howls like an over-eager cowboy; his seat falls away. It really does feel like flying. Yet he knows that's . . . what? He searches for the word. An illusion. A farce. Just like everything else he's ever done. Sure, he's been a celebrated "novelist." He's been awarded Bram Stokers and Silver Daggers, interviews with Katie Couric and Charlie Rose. But in truth? He's a glorified hack.

"John?"

He turns the wheel easily now. It's like a toy, one that tilts and creaks and makes funny sounds if you press the right buttons. *Look at me! Whee!* Just then he notices a woman on the hood. *At least I'm not her,* he thinks. Then his mind backs up. Wait. *There's a woman on the hood.* It's true, she's sliding around, trying to hold on, and only after a few seconds does he see the bleeding stumps where her hands ought to be and her ruined mouth forming blood-bubble words: *Why? Why did you do this to me?*

Am I already dead? he wonders. No. It's just a hallucination. He blinks her away. Still he has a creeping suspicion he knows her. Then it comes to him. Her name was—is—and always will be—Valerie. She's the first victim from his very first novel, the one he cried over as if she were real, having to remind himself she was just words on the page as he *carved* and *delineated* and *punctuated* her poor imaginary flesh. What does she want with him now? What is she telling him? There's something important here, but his mind can't grasp it. Panic is setting in. His hands are bathed in sweat. At any moment he'll be like her: a fiction, a dream. Is she counseling him to finally face his demons, the ones he's buried under mounds of make-believe? The pastiche of lies he calls his past, and what his novels *really* cost him to write?

Too late now. Snow studs the windshield. Wind whistles through tiny gaps where the windows meet the frame. He sets the wheel straight again, as if not doing this has been his mistake all along. He digs his thumbs into its grooves, telling himself an engineer actually thought of their perfect placement while he himself has only ever caused pain. He thinks of his two children, Milo and Klara, how he's damaged them, used them as *characters* in his own dark genre. At least this will be their freedom as much as his, a final gift to them.

They fly.

He is light, he is snow, a dangling participle, a story gathering momentum, a narrative's rising arc. He is the God of this Volvo's universe, and like any God he's enamored of the possibility of escape. The moon! He wants to go to the moon. Right there, looming beyond the clouds, a hazy yet somehow proximate place, a lifeless lunar glow. "Almost there," he says out loud. But his wife can't hear. She is laughing. Lines ripple across her rough rouged cheeks. She looks like she does when scolding him, telling him to *buck up* and *be grateful you have a public who adores you. No, not me,* he always wanted to say, *my books.* But even at the time he wasn't sure there was a difference. Now he reaches out to her. It's meant to be a final consolation, a way to say he's sorry. She flinches, pulls away. Because they're not going up anymore. Nor are they landing on a moon-crater. It's the ravine rushing toward them, faster than he thinks possible. He considers the ironic subtleties of grammar: what a difference it makes to transpose a single consonant and make a slight vowel shift.

They fall.

He's a child again. His father has just tossed him high into the air. Only it's not a soft-focus hazy happy kind of toss. His father wears a scowl and a white dress shirt drenched in pee. Johnny has done a VERY NAUGH-TY THING and now he's crying because he's just been hurled . . . No. He can change this. Re-write it. He can make his father jaunty and proud, like he ought to have been, can make him happy. *Why can't you write something happy instead of those awful horror books?*

He writes something happy. About falling into a young girl's arms. A redheaded Irish girl whose name he's long blocked from his mind. If only he can edit away the reason they met and why they had to love in secret, his British Army uniform and the terrible things he did to that girl's brother, which she could never know because then he'd have to . . .

Another flash. He's older now, holding Milo and Klara in his arms, telling himself he has a chance to do things right for a change, to break the cycle. It's a lovely summer's day. In America, the land of forgetting. A gust of wind rises up. Trees sway overhead, curious and dark. But he's keeping the darkness at bay with his proud smile, his loving arms, his bright white shirt and ruffled hair, his picture-perfect pose. *Don't move.* That's right. Freeze right there. Say *cheese.* A picture is worth . . . Stop.

The girl, the redhead. Her name was Blanaid. Meaning a *flower* or *blossom*.

Stop.

They're in his Army jeep, laughing. He punches the wheel. Suddenly the windshield explodes. He doesn't hear the bomb, but he knows what it must have been. He was so stupid to take her so far beyond the base. Now the jeep is on its side and her head is staved against the bolster and her smile's become a vacant unearthly bliss. Somehow he is alive. He begins to crawl away. There's a trail of blood on the pavement behind him. If only he can get to a phone . . . He stops to catch his breath. Best to slow down, observe what's happening. His blood is becoming absorbed into the ice. When the ice melts it will form a river to feed the hungry soil.

He snaps back to the present. The Volvo is a shattered wreck, a pointillist horror. Glass is everywhere, and he's lying facedown in the dirt, halfway out of the car. Snowflakes kiss his cheeks. Only one eye works. The other oozes down his cheek. Out of the corner of his good eye he glances back up, to the lip of the ravine. He sees headlights. The vague outline of a man peering down. A man with a checkered shirt, work boots, gloves, a shovel —a man he knows as well as his own children, a man who in a sense is his own child, too. Ever since seeing Valerie he's half-expected this. His own personal grim reaper. He's always loved the image of the reaper because that's what death is: the moment we turn from consumer to consumed—the moment we become food. Yet it's cold comfort now. He blinks. The man scuttles down the ice. Impossible with that sheer face, but he makes it look easy. *How?* he hears an old writing teacher say. *You've got to tell the reader how he can do the impossible.* But he can't. Suddenly he's scared, confused—this is all too real. Or is it? His brain screams *run.* He hears the thud of boots. The breathy pause. Just like he used to write it. He sees the shovel rise up like a stave, like an axe against the moon. The wind-whistle. *Let it come down.* It does. But not into him. Into the ice. Chips fly, glinting through the moon-reflected snow. The man quickly hits dirt. Hard as rock. He pries it loose, then begins tossing dirt onto him, onto the famous horror writer, whose one good eye quickly fills. It doesn't matter. With all the blood seeping in he can't see anyway, and doesn't have to, because he already knows what happens next.

Or so he thinks.

From the other side of the world he hears the man grunting, more soil scuttling across the shovel's blade. But on this side of the world he notices something else. A soft tickle in his ear. The intimate press of worm-flesh.

He knows this isn't real, just a premonition of what's to come, yet he's still surprised. The man shovels more dirt on top of him. The writer hears water sloshing in a bucket. Soon it comes trickling between his legs. He's about to die three ways—drowning, suffocating, and bleeding to death—when he finally realizes what's going on.

A memory comes to him, of watching Milo play behind the house, digging with a plastic shovel while he, the writer, watched, as he often did, taking notes on this strange lost boy while half-hidden behind a tree. Milo wore shorts and tall socks with red bands around the top, and he worked with a diligence that some took as a sign of mental slowness. His thin back was bent like a question mark as he dug a perfect rectangle. Then he sat down next to it. He seemed to contemplate his work. He had four wooden dolls laid out on the grass beside him. The dolls wore old-fashioned clothes—a man and small boy in green suits, a woman and girl in frontier-style dresses. Milo picked each one up and whispered something to it before stroking its bristly hair. He then placed them face-down into the hole, side by side, and when he was finished he stood and took up the shovel again and began covering them with dirt.

That's when the writer emerged from behind the tree, notebook still in hand. "What are you doing, Milo?"

The boy didn't look back, just answered as if talking to an idiot: "Gardening."

The word comes back to him now as he pictures where he is, inside this giant ravine, this furrow in the snow.

The man with the shovel and checkered shirt works carefully too, and the writer can feel the weight of the dirt atop him getting heavier, even as the water keeps trickling past. He tries to lift a hand. He can't. So he does the opposite, pushing down, his nearly dead weight pressing the snow, and to his surprise it gives way, there's a hole, he's punched clean through. Into what? He's heard glass shatter. He claws the air. He reaches deeper, up to his shoulder, feels the water trickle down his arm and drip from his fingers. He's grasping at something, anything, until he finds a curved plastic rod and pulls, hoping to escape that man yet, to yank himself down and miraculously out of harm's way, so he pulls until the rod rocks back and forth, and then he notices the grooves, which is his first sign that not everything is what it seems. Because it's not a rod at all. It's another steering wheel. There's a car beneath his own. It must have been buried lightly, on its side, at the bottom of the ravine. He lets go of the steering wheel. His arm swings back, into something delicate, something moist and soft and . . . Flowers? This surprises him more than anything he's encountered so far. How can flowers grow below ground? And in winter? For the moment he forgets his own pain, just thrusts his hand deeper into them, into their impossible caress, a last sensuous touch that nearly makes him cry, and that's when he comes upon the tangle of vines beneath the flowers. Trapped in the vines is something else, like a large silky tongue. He tugs. It doesn't come loose, it's wrapped around another thing, and when he slides his hand up it he can just feel the knot around the neck of it, and that's when he shudders, when he knows what this place is.

A garden.

And what his entire life has amounted to—what he's at last become.

A seed.

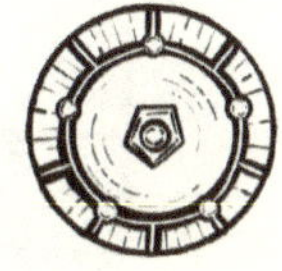

Landfall

~ Stephen O'Donnell

We were six hours rowin for shore and the current against us the whole time. Near shot from the effort. The bastard wind. And the houses along the shore shootin up smoke, burnin wild. Looked like the shores of hell. And the tanker already aground behind us, threatenin to bust her bows with every wave until finally she went with a less'n a groan in the final swell. We rowed on. The freezin spray and the skin of us windbitten, slaked raw by the brine and that fuckin knifewind. Laong wept when he set foot in that black sand. I near wept mysel. I had already given up, she said. Out there.

The station man nodded, said nothing.

So you'll see now that I hafta. She drained the cold dregs in her mug. She was sat naked and shivering before the muted glowing of the grate.

And is that where yous're going?

It is.

The station man stopped wringing the rag and shook his head. There's no turnin yous?

No, she said. There's an fuckin awful smell of it in here. Have ye a bad room?

Here? He shook his head. Don't even say that for a joke.

Well.

There's no fucking bad rooms in this place. The whole townlands has been gone over. Twice.

It's the smell of them, she said. In me mind. With the steam still rising from her she started to put back on the layers of her wet suit, checking the seals and diodes.

Don't use any main roads, the station man said.

Isn't it me own country?

No. Do you not see what they've done to the town?

I seen the fires.

Didn't that open your eyes?

To what?

If you don't fuckin know yet, I can't tell you. He slapped the rag into the filthy basin and turned and looked at her under the grimy kitchen light. You're a stranger to these, people. They are strangers to themselves. Heed me now. Keep to them backroads. The bog and the heather. Slice the hand of any that reach for you. It'll be upon you quicker than you think. Do you mind me?

I mind you, she said.

Would that you did. And fear them that approach you most of all. Open your eyes or have them rent open.

What is this? Who will go agin me out there?

You don't listen Aoiph. Everyone. Everyone. Just go if you're goin. That rain wont lift.

☉

They left before dawn with the light and unending rain all before them. She waited for Laong under the twisted remains of the viaduct. The country to the north sank and reappeared above the rain. She heard him squelching up the filthy alleyway to where she stood muddied to the hip, leaning against the stone archway.

Nary a fucking horses? Ye go the livery?

I went t'livery, yeah.

And he didn't have ary the one nag for sale? Aoipher spat into the mud. A delicate white line amid the black sludge. I'da took one between us.

Livery feller warn't there. They'd kilt'n eaten alla horses.

Mother of fuck.

Place's fulla bones. They had a fuckin donkey's arse hanging there, swinging in the breeze, and they was just carving strips off it when I walked in.

Have yer sling about ye?

Always.

Aoipher spat again. Lets hoof it then, she said. Don't trust ary the one of these bastards.

They set out into the dark of the day. A world of mud and sucking filth and the sparse trees and the grey sky the only break from the filth.

⊙

They climbed up out of the coastal flats and across the spongey treading of the bog road.

So many crows. Ever tree filled with the mockin bastards.

T'were never so bad before.

At a turnroad they saw the carcasses of a half dozen swans. The eyes eaten away. The innards burst, stomped to leather. Laong climbed the embankment and studied the dead birds. Aoiph, he said. The bastards've pressed this far.

Aoipher chewed a root and watched the smoke from a hut across the bog. No surprise. They'll be in every hole that's hidin a warm body from here on up.

Laong jumped back down into the wet mud. We make the croppings before dark?

This mud going? Chh. She spat the root into the dirt and then flattened it with her boot.

Well it aint no stroll Aoiphe. Ye wanna head back?

Quit usin my fuckin name out loud. Be bad if one of them get's aholt it.

Well, like I ast, what ye wanna do?

Aoipher trod on. There's the lesser ones, before the river. Won't be comfor'ble. Better'n going back, waitin for word to catch us up. After the word comes the doin.

☉

They moved on, Aoipher pushing her steps and the other meeting them without either speaking a word.

The road wound down into a dell and there were the beginnings of hedges and fallow fields. At a crest closest the village they paused, watching the small thatched cottages lit like pumpkins, the light faint and pulsing in the windowsquares. The day was failing.

Round, through the woods. Poachin man might hesitate to raise us.

Think we'd be stopped?

Fuckin sure, she said. Murdur ye fer the steel alone.

And them others, they might be about already?

Don't doubt that, Aoipher said. Not fer a second.

I'll chance the timber with ye.

They moved from the mud of the road and crept slowly among the stands of ash. Pausing in the mist like skittish deer. They kept the village to their bladesides as they moved in the falling darkness, under deadfall and over streambed, filthy and wet through by the time they gained again the common mire of the road. A hare ran screaming across the trail as they stepped into the mud. As it disappeared into the bracken a meteor broke the night air in a silent white shear.

No, Laong said. No.

Shurrup. Aoipher said. No time t'go slack. Get on. I know them lessers start soonabouts.

And they hurried up the road, away from the village.

Laong saw it first and gave a low shripes' whistle.

Twill hardly fit the hams of us, he said. But tis somethin glad all the same.

Aoipher pushed him in the shoulder. Get on, yer workbits.

When Laong had laid the patterns and uttered as he was bid, he climbed into the small concrete envelopment and stood chin to chin with Aoipher.

This is the night, Aoipher said.

A night it is, Laong said and he set out his elbows so that he might sleep standing.

Hares and shooting stars. Omens of the age.

☉

In the morning she woke to Laong watching her and watching the marshlands.

Ye can look till yer eyes are burnt, Aoiphe said.

No sign of 'em trackin us.

They're not given to leavin sign.

Sun's up I reckon, Laong said. They couldn't get at us.

There'll be dead down the village then.

We chance the road?

Aye, Aoipher said and she shunted him toward the entrance and then she followed him, gathering their webbing as she went.

☉

They moved along a narrow causeway. Sparse timber grew along the edge of the bog, drowned in ivy.

Alla birds is crow or rook. Not much of ary other in the trees. Reckon aught of the aviary made it ashore?

No, Aoipher said. I don't.

D'ya reckon any t'others made land?

Aoipher hiked on until she had to stop to catch her breath. Them, she said as she panted. Them I hopes drowned.

Magpies cackled somewhere down the ships corridors of her dreaming.

Do yeh think it has gotten hold of us yet?

Aoiphe shrugged. It don't come on fast. Until it does.

We're fuckin trapped, Laong said.

Details, she said. Details.

What?

Trapped and headin inta madness. What were the t'other choice? Sit with t'station man? Hope not to get rumbled, hopin someone hears the broadcast? That's only n'other type of fuckin madness.

It were them we heard, last night. Werent it?

Aye, Aoipher said. I thinkwise I did. Now take aholt of yerself. We've another week at this if that last reckonin aboard was right.

Whar if it wasn't? Whar if it were out?

I said take a fuckin hold of yer tongue. Hear me?

I'm hearin yeh.

We'll see how we fare. Day at a time. Recite t'me the landmarks. As they stood.

The shore. The beacon. The picking point. The decycle.

An then all the normal fuckin madness, Aoipher said.

Laong waved a hand at her. Don't talk namore bout madness.

Fine, Aoiphe said. Just ye recite that to yoursel the next time ye feel like gettin goin.

☉

The night found them inside an uncropped tier, large enough to sleep twenty men. They had to slice through a tight thicket of ivy to crawl inside.

A fire I reckon.

Aye, Aoipher said. Go on about yer ablutions. I'll fetch kindling.

Whar about the light?

It's nor a risk yet. Get about yer workins.

Laong dropped to his knees and twisted the nozzle below his collar. Aoipher climbed back into the crawl way, cursing against the grating of her suit in the darkness there.

Laong was almost finished and was turning water when he heard a sound in the crawlspace behind him.

A child led an immense man in a tin helmet into the room. They both paused when they saw Laong watching them.

Where'n, Laong said. Where'd ye come from?

The child, caked in mud, grinned. There is a crowd of them, the child said.

Whar?

A crowd. Yon next rise. And they are comin for ye both.

Laong looked at the man. Closed eyes and a closed mouth had been painted upon his helmet. Y'take off that bucket to see?

They know you are here, the child said. They know why you have come. Listen. They are taking your Aoiphe now.

Who told y'such things child? Laong said. Yer lummox does not bare a tongue?

Your iron boat. Landings are forbade. Any from the sea are to be drowned. Any from the sky to be burned.

This, this child speaks for you brute?

The painted eyes opened on the helmet and blinked once. A stream of breath snorted from the mouth.

Listen, the child said, pointing into the darkness behind Laong. Listen and you will hear.

Laong turned and screamed at what he saw.

☉

Aoipher heard Laong's scream. She cast the sods from her bad hand while the other cleared the rags from about the hilt of her steel as she moved quickly, staggering down from the bank into the road, stumbling, cursing the mud. She started fast up the trail.

☉

In the fray he lost sight of Aoipher. They dragged him off, chanting the whole while.

He did not know where he was, only that it was dark and there was a whutting sound like falling gobs of burning candle grease. He remembered. He remembered and knew from remembering. It was human fat they burnt. He remembered. *Fear their darkened rooms most of all.* He tried to move but his body shot with a cold pain that held him rooted. He could hear something stirring in the darkness beside him, where he could not see. He struggled to cry out but his jaw only trembled and refused to move. Only his eyes moved. He could see now what it was beside him and a strangled groan came from his rooted throat. He felt it seize him and he shrank from the teeth and the stench. His flesh burnt and finally his jaw sprang loose and he howled.

Getta fuckway from me. No, he hissed and he tried to move his arms but they were as stone. No no no no no. Tears streamed from his eyes and pooled ice cold in the back of his mask.

Laong ye stupid cunt, the dark thing said.

What, whatta fuck're yeh?

Laong you silly fucking cunt. It's me you fuck. The ablutions. Did ye finish the ablutions? Laong, it's important. The daemon lifted him and shook him hard. He shrank inside his mask at the face there, the face of Aoipher with a thousand teeth and the eyes that were not her own, eyes that burnt black fire.

No, Laong screamed and then he rose upwards into blackness.

☉

He woke lying on his side on the tier cement. Aoipher with her back to him, squatted on her haunches before a dying fire. All was pitchdark beyond the flames.

He sat upright painfully and shuffled closer to the fire.

Is it you Aoiphe?

Last time I lookt.

I dreamt, dreamt they took ye. Yeh tolt me they took ye.

Aoipher turned to look at him now. Speak it.

I dreamt we was kept in the dark together. And yeh told me they took ye.

The dream, what'd I say?

I can't remember.

Think.

How? How are you here? I seent them tear ye away, I had ye fixed for their fire. I saw yer face by the black light.

Tell it, Aoipher said.

You lookt kilt. *Yer face bloodied and the remains of yer great cloak in a rag about yer neck.*

Kilt, I said, you look kilt.

Those cunts, yeh said and then yeh spat onna floor. I aint near kilt. Not by that buncha, they had their hands about me and but I stuck two of em. Hard, inna chest.

And as you said it I heard the knife. The wound gurgling. The air loosed from some inner cavity.

Yeh grinned and said, Anat took some of the steam of t'others but they kept after me but at a distance now though I yet struck any I could reach, alla time backing down for the riverwaters I could hear someplace behind me in the darkness, slashing and stabbing and spitting at 'em and I only knew that if I made that fuckin water I'd be alright even though they'd stuck me, maybe twice.

I ast yeh, I said, did they bleed ye?

Aye, yeh said and yeh spat again, into the blackfire this time. Stung me a time or two in the dance of it. Such are the goings of a crater such as I, s'what yeh said and yeh laughed anat was a terrible laugh like it were inside my skull. Ye said: I will be dead before I'm taken blind by a posse of such calibre and you turned your face all wounded for me to see and I saw and and and and that's whar I remember, Laong said.

Wake up, Aoipher said and she threw a pebble at him.

I am, I am, I think.

Y'are now. Whatta the faces of the crowd? Aoipher said.

Nothing, faces. Faces with nothing left. They had great long haunched dogs all among them.

Hounds?

Aye, Laong said.

Had they markings?

Laong shook his head. Not that I'd see.

Dogs, Aoiphe said. Wild dogs. She shook her head. I aint a diviner. But that don't lie easy on me fuckin mind.

Throw on some more peat, Laong said. Please, I dreamt they was all amidst these woods.

They likely are.

Build it up Aoiphe. Please. I don't want one of them, them dogs to get any closer.

I aint heard naught, Aoiphe said. She picked up several small logs all the same and placed them on the bed of coals. The darkness receded. Fuck em. Let em come up again, purrit out with their own feet.

How do I know this is real?

Aoiphe shrugged. It's real. You been drivelling quite a time.

Laong snatched out a hand for the other's blade, touching the hilt.

Loosen it or swally the bitin end, Aoipher said. Be worse'n ary fuckin dream ye had.

Laong let his fingers fall and sat back. Aoipher dropped some peat to the flames now, pressed the twigs down and watched sparks crack and rise. Then she turned and looked at Laong.

It were more'n sleep then, Aoiphe said.

What?

They stopp yer ears?

Laong shifted on the ground slightly, slowly. He sneered with the effort.

Yer whalloped?

Feels so, Laong said. Is this its beginning?

Aoipher shook her head, and turned from the fire to the darkness. I don't know. Talkin bout it inna middle of the night won't do no good.

Are ye scairt?

You'd be too, y'had any fuckin sense.

When you had it. That first time, what were it like?

Aoiphe watched the fire a long time. No, she said. I won talk about it. Not after dark.

☉

At the first grey light that did not seem to grow any brighter Aoipher was shuffling about, a strange fire in her blood.

Laong watched her from his bedroll. Should we plan t'way some more?

No, she said, blinking as she grubbed sleep from her eye. We just get foot under road. Kick out that fire, gather what pieces're left ye.

Goin agin? Shouldn't I rest some?

No. I aint havin m'throat cut be no halfwit baker boy. Today, I'm goin and goin. We're too slow. The muck out there. Aoipher said and then she stood over the fire and spat phlegm into the ashes.

☉

They moved over a series of low cliffsides, thick with bri-arforest and the waves constant against the cliffside in a sound that shook in their lungs.

Are ye moulting? Yer rancid.

Laong didn't answer. He stared at the black mud as they walked. The mud pulsed slightly, slowly, as if the earth were possessed of some latent bloodpulse. He could feel it in his suitsoles when the soil rose and sank. He looked up at the treeline and shook his head and then he looked at the mud again. The mud began to coil and sluice in strange cords, separating and rejoining.

Wharssat?

Aoiphe looked at where he was pointing. Hah?

The mud. It's the fuckin mud.

Mud an' shit's all I've seen since we come aground. I hate this fuckin trail and ever cunt upon it.

Later black rot worms rose from the churning mud. Laong stepped upon them viciously and their blood ran black as any man's.

Worms, he said. Them're fucking bloodworms.

What?

Fucking worms and serpents, he said. For they were now a cold writhing mass of snakeheads, curling in a silent mulch about his boot, covering the ground before him. He drew his dagger and held it unsteadily. A dark flame burned along the blade's edge. He waved it before him. It left faint trails in the air.

Y'see it?

Wha? Are yeh fuckin senseless?

Black fire, Laong said. D'ya see it? How the steel burns. See? He swung the dagger in small vicious circles.

The balms, Aoiphe said. Quickly. Have ye the last of ye balms? Where've yeh them hid, she said as she clutched hold of Laong. Where?

Whar?

Aoiphe pulled at Laong's capsule pockets. Idjit, we're done for.

I have buried them in darkness.

Aoiphe slapped him. Fuckin listen to me. Speak fuckin sense. Nightfall, the bastards in the woods. Remember, she said and she slapped him again. The landmarks. Remember t'fuck.

I, what, Aoiphe what've yeh aholt of me fir?

The parcels, the blutions.

Yea, they're, they' someplace, here. Here. Me heartpocket. Fill em. Fill em.

Oh, Laong said. We need water for that. Mineral mechanisms're part spent.

Wha? Spent? Why'n fuck didn't ye say this morn? Fuck. She studied the treeline before them. I seent common road again, a while back. There were some thatch.

Kin we risk it?

We've no fuckin choice, Aoipher said. Won't never make it with spent balms.

You said not tay panic.

Come on ta fuck, who sez I am? Step quickly, we kin repluck our way, unfuck oursels, find their well, or a stream maybe.

☉

They came up through a cut in the backwoods and could see the thatch roof huge among the maples.

The trough, Aoipher said. Mark it? Near covered over, see the smooth stone of it?

Kin we risk it?

No choice now. Get tay it.

Laong hurried from the brush and stooped to rewater with the nozzle in his hand. Aoipher kept watch of the inn door. Two mules were tied to a sunked post. Voices from an upper room, drunken giggling. When Aoipher looked back Laong was drinking ravenously from cupped hands, leering at his own grimy face as he swallowed in huge, sucking gulps.

Wharra fuck are ye doing, Aoipher hissed. Fill yer balmcups.

Whattad ye know bout it? Laong filled his dipper cups and struggled with them back into the shelter of the timber.

Willit take long?

Laong shook his head. Leave me mix what needs mixin.

Aoipher stood on a rock and watched the door of an inn.

She saw the door open and a man emerge at a run, grabbing at the hitches of his trousers as he waddled toward them.

Gucka fuggin pishh, the man gasped. Fugg.

Aoipher crouched down.

What is it?

Be still, she said. Say naught, locals.

The man came into the copse, pissing as he walked, laughing at the steam havoc he created upon the dead leaves, his eyes like nacre. His stream dried to a trickle that stained his filthy pants as he saw them crouched like upended hatchlings.

The man grinned down at them. Maken pudden?

Aoipher stood, wiping her hand along herself and nodding at the man.

Together, srrange. Dressed for paegent? Assa good get-up. Assa gud wan. Shrink?

Laong looked at Aoipher. Whars he say?

Aoipher raised a hand behind her back. Shrink'd be kindly, she said and she made a shape in the air with her other hand.

The man looked down at Laong and rubbed his head. That ya goslin?

Aye, aye.

The man shrugged again and pushed his penis back into his pants. Mon that shrink so, he said and turned back for the inn.

Wharre yah doin?

Say naught, Aoipher said and she walked after the man toward the inn. Foller me lead.

Just fuckin drop im.

Say fucking naught. He'd have a posse on us, we refuse. C'mon.

They stepped through the doorway and into the greasy

light of the inn.

Ese're bound a'paegent. Coming a con a shrink from me, the man said and he laughed.

Two forms in rags at a huge hearth nodded and then turned away the newcomers. The man led them to a bench and waved them to sit. He pushed two crudely hollowed pieces of wood toward them. From the floor he lifted a flagon and unstoppered it and filled their wooden mugs.

Shrink, shrink, shrink, the man said. He watched them regard the liquid. Then Aoipher took the cup and drank quickly. She looked at Laong.

Gettit over weh, Aoipher said.

Laong took it and sipped quickly and then he sat back in the chair shaking.

☉

What is it you mudsliders are come about?

Come about? Hear this cur bark?

It's nay from the like of ye I'll low such talk.

Step to with steel so, Aoipher shouted and she had her own drawn and red in the firelight.

Laong pressed his arm across Aoipher's shoulder. Not in here. Y'see him but ye don't see the others behind'm, watchin ye. He pulled Aoiphe backwards to the bench. Sit. Take s'more. Puttat fuckin steel 'way. He lifted a mug to the other table. Sit or they'll stamp the wind from yeh.

☉

They came staggering from the hedge in the slow grey light of dawn.

Aoipher pushed the other. Y'stink, she said. Ye need dunking.

Get on pissbody.

Foul, Aoipher said. Even for a roadgoer. Get a dunk or lop off me nose.

I'll lop it easy, the other said and he tripped and fell flat in the mud.

We should nort have drunk 'at water.

Nor stayed inna keepers bed.

I slept in nay bed.

Pah. A skeet of spittle shot from between Laong's bucked teeth. I'd do that twice agin for half of naught. Dirty aul cunt, all I wanted was something to rub up against.

Y'blistered bastard. Have ye, well have ye yer edged edge about ye at least?

Awluss. Awluss. Man says theys a fair up these roads someplace.

Wha man? Station man?

Whar? Naw, Laong said. Naw. Inn feller. So he says as I were lacing mysel up. Him lying pink and raw. Only talk truth whenat they's leeched raw.

Aoipher stopped suddenly and turned to look at the empty road behind them. *She heard a voice call her name over her shoulder, birdsong in a twisting tunnel, roaring silent through the black void far from any soil and the voice calling remember remember remember from the twisting darkness.*

See sommat? Deer?

I thought, she said. A name? Maybe? Naw, she said and she hiccupped and fell laughing to her knees. I'm hearing voices. She began to laugh and then she began to weep. I'm hearing fucking voices.

Laong pulled her by the arm. It's the grog. Brainrot. Gerrup. Mon. S'more'll see ye right, he said and then he staggered away from the road and into the briars to piss.

Laong, staggering back to the mud, wiping mud upon himself. Feller said watch out for 'em ditchsnakes.

Feller?

Taverner fella. He'll be a few coin short.

Aoipher took up step beside Laong. Ye loosened his load?

Never in a dell. He shook his finger solemnly. He'll only be walking gammy a time. Won't be no poorer.

He might be met yet.

He might. The roads are wild things, filled with madmen, Loang said and he began to cough. Who's to say the misfortunes as a man might meet?

They stumbled on, down toward the carnivalgrounds. Through the trees they could see the bonfire, huge and roaring, now vesper green, now a crackling blue. Aoipher tottered at the edge of the treeline and stood watching. She saw the ones who were gathered, saw their faces were as the faces of lizards and their feet were shod as the feet of bulls and all around the flames they murmured together in low whispers like the whispered workings of maggots and now they had all turned to watch her and she knew it was her name they were whispering.

Wasn't there somethin we was, Aoipher hissed, clutching wildly at Laong. A boat?

About? A bout whar? Boot fer a foot? Or a shoe fer a pony? Laong giggled. Wasn't naught we had to do but get on to yon fairground. Theys all waiting on us.

VI

The Continuing (Superpositional) Adventures of Schrödinger's Cat

~ David Hewitt

Erwin Schrödinger's famous feline thought experiment on quantum uncertainty should require no introduction. As a quick refresher, Schrödinger himself expounded it thus:

> . . . A cat is penned up in a steel chamber, along with the following device . . . in a Geiger counter, there is a tiny bit of radioactive substance, so small, that perhaps in the course of the hour one of the atoms decays, but also, with equal probability, perhaps none; if it happens, the counter tube . . . releases a hammer that shatters a small flask of hydrocyanic acid. If one has left this entire system to itself for an hour, one would say that the cat still lives if meanwhile no atom has decayed. [Until an observer opens the chamber] the psi-function of the entire system would express this by having in it the living and dead cat (pardon the expression) mixed or smeared out in equal parts.

Recent theoreticians, however, consider Schrödinger's formulation over-simplistic. Before the box is opened, the cat cannot be said to exist "smeared out" over only the two states—alive and dead. Rather, this daring hypothetical adventurer simultaneously exists, with varying statistical likelihood, in every conceivable state of its own wave function. What follows is a by-no-means-exhaustive summary of possible outcomes, and hence co-existing states of being, revealed by continuing analyses of "the cat problem":

• An atom decays; the hammer strikes the flask of hydrocyanic acid; the cat dies of cyanide-induced histotoxic hypoxia.

• An atom does not decay; the hammer does not strike the flask of hydrocyanic acid; the cat does not die of cyanide-induced histotoxic hypoxia and lives happily and healthily to a ripe old age.

• An atom does not decay during the one hour; but in the name of thoroughness and replicability, the scientist repeats the experiment the next day. This time, an atom does decay and—hammer, cyanide—the cat dies.

• An atom does not decay on the first day, nor when the experiment is repeated on the second, nor even on the third; but on the fourth day, though the clear and present odds are still a simple 50/50 coin toss, the cumulative 15-to-1 odds

against surviving four such coin tosses in sequence finally
catch up with the cat and . . . hammer, cyanide—dead.

• The cat survives the first, the second, the third, and
even the fourth day. On the fifth day, the scientist, who
originally intended an even five experimental trials, has
a change of heart. Just as the atom is decaying, she hurls
open the door of the steel chamber and, as the hammer
is falling, yanks the subject out and tumbles to the floor
with cat cradled in her arms, saved in the nick of time
from the grim clutches of cyanide-induced histotoxic hypoxia. The scientist takes the cat home, names her Prin-
cess Purrsnickitty, and the two live happily ever after.

• The scientist experiences no change of heart, but just
as the cat is being placed in the steel chamber, a joint
PETA/Animal Liberation Front strike team armed with
crowbars bursts into the laboratory, and liberates the cat
into the uncertainties and vast open spaces of the subur-
ban wilds.

• Just as the cat is being placed in the steel chamber,
not animal-rights commandos but an ASPCA lawyer
sporting a stodgy suit, a questionable comb-over, and a
restraining order bursts into the laboratory, and liberates the cat into the uncertain and vastly time-consum-
ing and expensive vagaries of the United States judicial
system.

• Just as the cat is being placed in the steel chamber, neither PETA/ALF commandos nor ASPCA advocate but rather two blue-tufty-haired, red-jumpsuited individuals burst into the laboratory. Running full tilt and wreaking general havoc by toppling sensitive equipment, a coffee maker, and even a fish bowl, they free the cat through happenstance from the steel chamber and flee. Because of the suspects' breakneck speed, blurry security footage provides only one lead: a single frame in which the cryptic letters *-ing 1* and *-ing 2* can be discerned on the backs of the jumpsuits.

• Just as an atom is about to decay, the cat reaches into a magic fourth-dimensional pocket on his belly and extracts an "Anywhere Door"; he transports himself out of the steel chamber and into the bedroom of a young Japanese boy who, though receptive to the cat's aid and tutelage, never masters the important life lessons the cat endlessly strives to impart.

• The atom does not decay; the cat will live another day, it seems—but wait! Just as the chamber is opened, a gleeful-looking Maya-blue mouse rushes into the laboratory, carrying a giant drill and a hose with a suction cup at one end. The mouse drills his way into the steel chamber, slaps the suction cup onto the cat's muzzle, squeezes cartoonishly through a hole into the perforated box where the flask of cyanide sits, screws the other end of the hose to the mouth of the cyanide flask, and flips the hammer's trigger with a white-gloved hand. The hammer smushes the flask, squeezing all the cyanide out as a visible bulge which travels up the hose, through the suction cup, and into the cat. The cat turns a grotesque shade of green and its eyes a jaundiced yellow, then its fur and skin melt from its bones, and the bones themselves dissolve into a steaming puddle of acid with a pair of yellow eyes lolling on top. The mouse kicks one then the other eye, shot-on-goal style, and scampers off in the height of good cheer.

• An atom decays; somebody erred, however, and, in place of hydrocyanic acid, filled the flask with rye whiskey. When the hammer strikes the flask, the cat, goaded by the stress of its captivity, laps up the rye. Outside the sealed steel chamber, the scientist, who can know nothing of all this, takes a glass flask from his pocket and sips. He could swear he'd filled it with rye this morning, but the mouthful he sips has a distinctly non-whiskey, almond-like flavor.

• An atom decays, but rather than triggering the hammer, the ionizing radiation flies in another direction and collides with a spider which, unbeknownst to anyone, crept into the steel chamber before the experiment began. Bitten by this spider, said cat gains the spider's proportional strength and agility (the latter resulting— since arachnid agility rates much lower than that of family *felidae*—in a net agility loss). The cat uses this super-strength to break free from its captivity, and goes on to fight for cat-truth, cat-justice, and the Siamese way.

• An atom decays; the cat is poisoned and dies, and is buried unceremoniously under a rock. On the third day, though, the rock is miraculously rolled aside—the cat, licking itself, rises from the grave as savior to all catkind, having paid with its suffering for the original sin of the first cat-ancestors, Muffin and Max, who selfishly tasted of the catnip of the Tree of Sloth and Hyperactivity.

• An atom does not decay, but neither does the cat live to a ripe old age. Instead, loose in the neighborhood, it is run over by a car the very next day—but the bereft scientist inters it in an ancient Native American burial ground. Two days later, the scientist hears a scratching at his door, and either does or does not open it; in either case, his own story ends in a manner that may with 93.2% probability be described as "bloodcurdling."

• Just as the cat is being placed in the steel chamber, not PETA/ALF commandos, not ASPCA advocates, not red-jumpsuited hooligans, but rather a wealthy private benefactor arrives at the laboratory to rescue the feline, offering a generous research stipend in compensation. This benefactor, an older gentleman in tweed jacket and wrinkled trousers, brings the cat home. Soon after, a meeting is arranged with an editor from a major publishing house. The result is *Eight More Lives: My Journey Through the Steel Chamber* (ghostwritten). The hardcover release hits #6 on *The New York Times* Best Seller list and paves the way to the cat's starring on the popular but horribly ill-conceived reality show *Pussies and Pitbulls*. Against all odds, our hypothetical feline hero emerges victorious, leaving a trail of savaged canine bodies in her wake. But she is a changed cat—hardened, unstoppable, eyes blazing with plutonium potency and heart hell-bent on revenge. Against all her benefactor's protestations, the cat gives herself over once again to science, this time volunteering for a ludicrously improbable time-travel experiment. The experiment succeeds, transporting the cat a century into the past. Through hard-won cunning and craft, this survivor among survivors, this titanium-willed tiger among tabbies, makes her way to her target. The next morning, a young Erwin Schrödinger is found dead in his bed—of histotoxic hypoxia. No evidence of forced entry or a struggle is found. In fact, Schrödinger's demise, mere days before he formulated his famous paradox, renders the existence of the thought experiment, the cat, and this story alike—

(With a 99.967% probability, very likely) The End

A Pamphlet Found Among Broken Glass Near the East Wing

Entrance

~Jonathan Raab

The Orford Parish Historical Society welcomes you to the Marvel Whiteside Parsons Memorial Mall and Food Court! This pamphlet's production and printing costs are generously funded by a partnership between the Historical Society, the Orford Parish Downtown Improvement District, and mall property owner, Malthus Retail and Correctional Services, Inc.

Since being built in 1972 by local labor—just like Revenant's Finger Middle School slogan says: "Orford Parish Breeds for the Labor Pits!"—and designed by an architect and suspected occultist whose name was struck from the blueprints, the Parsons Memorial Mall has been a center of commerce, culture, and alternative aerospace research for almost 50 years.

Upon first glance, Parsons Memorial Mall may seem like it has seen better days—what with the majority of its storefront units rendered abandoned by the predations of global capital, the rats, the imminent structural failure of a large portion of its roof system, the ever-present blood in the central fountain, the rats that *crawl and squeak like human babies*, the theft of the Moroni the Angel mannequin from the tableau depicting various secret and nefarious Masonic rituals brought out every Lenten season, the strange and malignant whispers that only cancer survivors working the closing shift can hear, the rats that *think* and *talk* and *parlay with the goat-legged sorcerer who appears nightly at the edge of the wood*, and the ominous radiological phenomena around the second floor men's bathroom (mentioned in FOIA-acquired and heavily redacted Air Force documents from Project WILL-O-WISP)—despite all this and more, we can assure you that the mall's best days are yet to come!

That's why we have authored this one-of-a-kind pamphlet and tour guide to this historic and beloved community institution. As part of a mysterious and generous state grant offered by a bureaucrat from Away whose face and voice none could recall save through their inexplicable and invasive presence in traumatic memories of car accidents that never occurred, this pamphlet and guide was commissioned to bring a little of the Mall's history to life for shoppers, local history buffs, and wayward tourists who pulled off the highway for gas and have found themselves unable to navigate the labyrinthine roads to find an escape. No matter how many maps they consult or how loud they scream and beg with the invisible, indifferent idiot-god that has made their lives a living hell, they will not be permitted to leave until the *Proper Time.*

If you happen to be one of those unlucky souls trapped in a space-time loop that refuses to release you from our quirky and historic city—welcome to your new home! Please contact the Historical Society to get recommendations on our many affordable abandoned home properties scattered throughout the hollowed out remains of our once-vibrant municipality. It's a buyer's market!

Although built in the early 1970s over the razed remains of an impoverished and largely ethnic neighborhood colloquially referred to as "the Mick Warrens," the history of the site goes far beyond the cyclical displacement and disenfranchisement of minority groups that define Orford Parish's Nietzschean gyre through dead and haunted time. In a collection of documents housed in one of our beloved Historical Society's many FORBIDDEN ROOMS there are accounts of hometown Revolutionary War hero and accomplished serial murderer Eli Elderkin himself negotiating for the town's purchase of the land from a local American Indian tribe that refused to have its name written on "cursed Orford parchment, lest we find our souls drawn to one of the white man's deranged hells."

Elderkin had made a study of the ley lines intersecting throughout Orford Parish and identified the low hill where the mall now sits as a "conflu'ense of forces malign and untapped." The anonymous tribe had been using it as a burial ground, but were eager to quit the land surrounding Orford Parish and happily took Elderkin's meager initial offer and departed for Canada. According to tradition, they cautioned Elderkin to "mind the cairns and see that water is never drawn from that blighted hill."

Eli, emboldened against curse-work by his pact with some foul pig-headed devil of the lowland hills, promptly secured town funds to hire local laborers (read: the Irish) to clear the stacked rocks and piled deer antlers marking the hill's many graves, but left the bodies of the tribesmen buried beneath, "that their bones might be the pillars upon which our white man's imperial domain is built." Now you know where the mall's motto comes from!

As for the water. Management tore out all of the drinking fountains in 1974, yes, but that was part of a boarder, city-wide project to discourage feckless hydration among the city's ill-constitutioned youth. It had nothing to do with the appearances of a stone statue of dog-headed St. Christopher the Cynocephalic throughout the property the year prior. That was most likely due to the personal moral failings of our city council, not to contaminated water, although the symbolic synchronicities are not lost on this committee.

Elderkin led the parish's efforts to construct what his blood-encrusted personal papers refer to as "The Black Longhouse," but his death in 1793 halted construction. For several decades later, as the village limits grew closer and closer to that sloped and damnable hill, drunks and impure Catholic children reported seeing processions of "befoul'd emerald fairie lites" at certain unholy times of year, often appearing with dwarven, blue-faced hooded figures gathered to commune with witches and syphilitics among the abandoned pillars of Elderkin's unfinished dread longhouse.

Parish records resume mentions of the site again in 1837, when the deed was purchased by one Genesee

Dryden of Rochester, who, having quit the Empire State and his failed career as a human taxidermist, decided to seek his fortune in Orford Parish as an amateur apothecarist and whoremonger. Dryden oversaw the clearing of the ruins and built his cathouse-of-medicine upon the very same diseased earth. He is credited with the precursor to Orford Parish's first public housing projects, having built a series of rowhouses for his female employees for when they were off-duty and in the blissful embrace of high-potency opium. The Whore's Hill Recreation Center gets its name from this industrious chapter of Parish history!

Our beloved Parish's growth, spurred on by the licentiousness of its vaguely European doggerel ethnics, soon reached and subsumed the outpost. From the latter half of the 19th century to that of the 20th, the hill was, at various times: home to multiple disenfranchised immigrant communities driven to American shores by an imperial war machine that blindly drinks blood and sows chaos; a hotbed of fringe religious and political activity; the site of ghastly exsanguinations occurring off and on over a thirty-year period that continues to drive troubled police detectives to madness; ground-zero for an anti-natalist plot to overthrow the government of these United States; selected to host the American Eugenics Movement Conference of 1967; home to the First, True, and Ever-Present Mall; and was prominently featured in a number of unaired UFO documentaries produced by disgraced quack and noted promise-breaker "Doctor" Jacques Vallee.

"The entire city is an open sewer of satanic ufological phenomena," Jacques? Really?

The construction and opening of the Marvel Whiteside Parsons Memorial Mall and Food Court in 1972 is perhaps the damnable hill's proudest hour. The multi-winged, multi-storied monstrosity has been studied in architectural programs the world over as a cautionary tale of the hubris of man, and has been home to a number of great retail outlets over the years, including Sears, K-Mart, Target, Macy's, Electronics Boutique, Suncoast Motion Picture Company, Media Play, Spencer's Gifts, Victoria's Secret, Foot Locker, and the best fast food restaurants that can be found wherever our brave boys and gals in uniform bring democracy and freedom.

Occupancy rates are down 70% since the self-implosion of American industry during the decades-long death crawl of post-war capitalism, of course, but many fine stores still remain open for your shopping pleasure! Here's just a few of the great establishments ready to serve you here at the Parsons Memorial Mall!

Polygonal Dreamwares
Owned and operated by Barret Carmile—a local man inexplicably still interested in electronic distractions for small children and the mentally deficient, and who is therefore disqualified from other fields of employment reserved for virile and self-sufficient men—Polygonal

Dreamwares is Orford Parish's premiere one-stop shop for all of the latest video games and systems. In addition to the hottest titles and big releases, Mr. Carmile's public shrine to his own masculine inadequacies features a wide variety of "retro" games and consoles from generations past. The back room features a number of unique and rare items for those unfortunate degenerates self-identifying as video game "collectors." Working prototypes, homebrew carts, and copies of banned, satanic, heretical, illegal, madness-infused, and reality-breaking collections of forbidden code occupy these shelves, waiting to corrupt and metastasize human brains with waves of paranoia-inducing graphics, flashing lights, and horrific electronic sound effects tuned to the frequencies of dying pulsars in deep space.

Anne Gare's Rare Books & Ephemera II
The first (and only, to date!) expansion location of our sister city Leeds' original shop, founded in an abortive effort to cash in on the hot retail-chain-bookstore craze of 2009, Anne Gare's Rare Books & Ephemera II is the best place this side of the Ron Paul School of Medicine on 5th Street to find a summer potboiler, the latest pathetic self-help bestseller, or a moldering tome writ in blood describing the true occult history of the United States. Here you can find rare and out-of-print titles such as a first edition of the infamous proto-Gothic horror

novel *The Crypt of Blood* by Countess Blair Oscar Wil-
flame, an original, fire-damaged screenplay of *Behold the
Undead of Dracula* pulled straight from the smoking ruins of Camlough Studios in Northern Ireland, and the
flesh-bound *A Grimoire of Dark Magic as Revealed by
the Lesser Swamp Gods of Little Dixie.* The owner is a bit
old-fashioned—dressed as he/she is in limitless, flowing
purple robes, face hidden behind impenetrable folds of
darkness, her/his voice the tenor of repressed childhood
traumas—so be sure to bring your standard American
Petrodollars, as this nightmare-made-flesh only accepts
cash! (Or Innsmouth gold.)

The Media Graveyard

An eclectic, solitary boutique housed in the other-
wise-abandoned east wing, the Media Graveyard features
row upon row of vinyl records which, this Society has
learned, have come back "in style" once more, yet again
proving the infallible thesis of mathematician and mis-
understood genius Dr. Gene Ray's (PBUH) Time Cube
theory. Used DVDs and Blu-Rays, paperback pulp novels, stacks of VHS tapes, vintage board games, and more
are piled high to the water-damaged ceilings, forming
what the regulars refer to as THE IMPOSSIBLE LABY-
RINTH, into which more than our fair share of missing
pets, children, and the elderly have wandered into, only
to return days, weeks, months, or even years later, pos-

sessed of some nightmarish intelligence that accurately predicts the geometric dispositions of the crop circles appearing in the fields of frustrated local farmers every fall. There's also an espresso machine.

The Food Court

A selection of local and chain stores so vast and terrible that none born of woman may know its true limits or majesty. Behold, in flashing neon signage and blinking electronic screens, *behold*, in the rising steam of frying meats and meat byproducts, *behold*, in the sugary embrace of death hidden in each gulp of corn syrup-laced drink, behold, in the capitalist illusion of upward mobility flickering in the dead-eyed stares of middle aged adults working dead-end fast food jobs, **BEHOLD**, in the horrors of our class system, of our Mammon-worshipping business caste's indifference to the quality and quantity of food produced through an inhumane (but truly human) agricultural system that destroys the earth, the animals, the plants, and the very people who produce and consume it, **B E H O L D** America itself, laid bare and spread-legged for all to see her shame, her nakedness, her rotten and pestilence-ridden touch upon a holy earth created and consecrated by God Himself for our failed stewardship. Woe, woe unto man! Who in his hubris and lust might produce such soul-rending terrors, who might visit such violence against the birds of the air and the beasts of the earth and the creatures of the sea, all in the name of the demon-gods Convenience and Quarterly Profits. Woe! Woe, unto thee, dear visitor, for the cabal of goblins that infest this satanic charnel house seek to slake your thirst and satiate your hunger through their Value Menu delights! Frolic in pink slime, chicken nuggets be thine!

The Store That Has No Name but That Will Appear in the Dreams of Those Touched by the Gods of Dust
(You struggle to focus on the text but find it unreadable, the letters and words jumbled and twisting just out of sight. You can't read this section of the pamphlet yet. But you will. When the time is right.)

The Orford Parish Outdoors Superstore
Need supplies for hiking, camping, fishing, or hunting? The OP Outdoors Superstore has you covered! Featuring high-quality gear at reasonable prices, you can stock up on supplies before hitting the woods this weekend. Considering the per capita rate of disappearances in the unmapped wilderness surrounding Orford Parish is the highest in the nation (outside of our terrifying National Park system, of course), having a few extra supplies and the right equipment is a good idea for regional outdoor recreators! The su-

perstore also features the largest selection of for-sale fire-
arms in the state, rivaled only by the militia encampment
and open-air weapons market outside of town. We've
even gone so far as to beg for assistance from the state
police for help with them, but it turns out many such
officers are members of the American Templar Sovereign
State themselves and are quite unwilling to dislodge their
fellow armed racists from their fortified redoubt.

```
Malthus  Alternative  Aerospace  Research
Labs and Anomalous Atmospheric Phenomena
Data Collection Station 6

Remote Viewer: MB
Interviewer: TB
Observers: JR, SMT, JP, SJB, TC
Date: 08/23/19
Starting Time: 1143 hours, local
Site #: MAARLAAP DCS6
Site Acquisit.: PVD RI
Working Mode: OG
Ending time: 1151 hours, local
Highest Stage: 8
Actual Site: Arapaho National Forest, CO.
SECOND SITE UNKNOWN
RV Summary: WENDIGO 4

TRANSCRIPT BEGINS AS FOLLOWS
```

TB: We have given you the coordinates. Please go to that location.

MB: Okay.

TB: What do you see?

MB: It's sort of a large space. Big, but full of something. Maybe half-empty?

TB: Please affix yourself to these coordinates, and these coordinates specifically, and describe what you see from that location.

MB: I'm sorry, it's like there's a current here. Is this—moving water? Like a river? No, that doesn't—there are tall—okay, trees? I get the impression that I'm very tiny. Like I'm small, and everything around me is—trees. Okay, this is a forest. I see a hill, across—across a road. The reason I didn't realize they were all trees at first is because they're skeletal. Grey. A fire's been through here. I don't know much about forest fires, but it looks like some trees are okay and some are knocked over but there's a lot of grey ones, burnt up.

TB: Please sketch out what you see from your perspective. Build a terrain map as best as you can.

MB: Yeah, I'd like to, but I get the feeling I'm in that river—that I'm being pulled—[INCOMPREHENSIBLE]. Jesus Christ. Jesus Christ.

TB: What's happening?

MB: I'm moving. Going somewhere else.

TB: Please remain at these coordinates.

MB: I can't. Please. I can't. I don't want to go.

TB: Remember your breathing techniques.

MB: They're not—they're not letting me. They know I'm here. They saw me immediately. I couldn't get—

TB: Please return to the coordinates.

MB: Saw me before I even went to the forest. Felt me. They've taken me someplace else. Said there's something I should see.

[Cross-talk. A third voice speaks inaudibly from the control room.]

TB: Okay, we want you to go with it now.

MB: Go with them.

TB: Okay. Where are they taking you? What can you see?

MB: It's . . . red, here, brown. Rust-colored. Rust everywhere. Like a desert, but deeper than that, you know?

TB: What do you see? Can you generate any numbers for coordinate sequencing?

MB: I can, yes, but it's not in USGS format. The alphanumeric strings are—

[An unidentified voice from the control room says the phrase "off world."]

MB: Right, that's what I was—the sense I was getting. I'm on a plateau. There's a canyon below. They're pointing toward the canyon.

TB: What do they look like?

MB: They won't let me see. I try to look at them but they get angry. I get the impression of teeth. I don't know if they have teeth, or if they are using the image of teeth to communicate threat or displeasure. I can't tell.

TB: Try.

MB: They're going to hurt me. They're going

to hurt me if I don't do as they say. They want me to look into the canyon. There's something there they're trying to show me.

TB: I need you to look at them. We need a description.

MB: They're saying that they will not let you see [REDACTED]. They'll never let you see. They will show you what they have to show you.

TB: Don't break the connection. Okay, look into the canyon, but try to—

UNKNOWN SPEAKER: Your walls of concrete cannot protect you. Your plutonium cannot protect you. Your procedures and your rituals are inadequate. They are merely vectors for our emergence.

TB: Terminate connection, remove the DMT drip.

[Metallic sounds, a low hum, a grinding noise. The sound of a pistol cocking.]

END TRANSCRIPT.

◇

Bethy's Pretzel Stand and Cell Phone Kiosk
The scent of cinnamon, butter, and baking dough can be smelled all throughout the north wing of the mall—and that's thanks to Bethy's Pretzel Stand and Cell Phone Kiosk! Grab a quick snack or an untraceable burner phone from a man who speaks with an incomprehensible guttural accent, and who is constantly shouting at someone on his own phone when not engaged with a customer. The wall you can see behind him is home to a door. A door that opens to a large, empty white room, where all of your personal failings, embarrassments, and sexual frustrations are projected onto the walls and ceiling. A sitcom audience laugh track groans and boos and chuckles in concert with your many inescapable shames.

Gustav's Surveillance and Home Security Emporium
What home in Orford Parish is complete without a series of byzantine and impenetrable locks on the door that leads to the Tunnels? How does one feel safe without a grainy, closed-circuit television system installed in the secret reaches of their house or apartment? Need porch cameras to capture footage of the strange, string-like beings that stalk through your lawn at night? What about audio equipment to record the secret whispers in the ventilation system spoken in the voice of your dead grandmother? Gustav, ex-Spetsnaz paratrooper, has you covered! Top-shelf military- and police-grade surveil-

lance equipment is flooding the market and cheaper than ever, thanks to our society's horrific police state apparatus. Also available are Gustav's signature gold-foil plated helmets, designed to prevent extraterrestrial mind-wave interference and decrease the rate of those nightmarish abduction experiences so many of us in the Parish have been suffering since puberty. He's only sold a few so far, and the reviews have been mixed—but every purchase helps fund further research. Keep tinkering away, Gus!

We hope you'll enjoy your time here at the Marvel Whiteside Parsons Memorial Mall and Food Court. You have of course by now realized that while the exits from the mall are all clearly marked, leaving Orford Parish itself is another thing altogether. The roads may yet disentangle and let you leave—as they have been known to on nights like tonight, when the ley lines' terrible occult energies wane—but the mall itself will remain lodged in your memory, a siren calling you back in thought and dream. And call you back it will, to this time, to this place, over and over again.

The Eurasian swastika shape of the mall's design was meant to be a defense against the malignant forces at work deep beneath the soil of our beloved Parish. But even unenlightened outsiders From Away eventually realize that symbols of light-aligned forces are meager defense against the seething will of That Which Dreams

Beneath. You must see now that, even if you do leave and somehow manage to carve out a full and meaningful life somewhere else in this hellscape of a rotting empire, a piece of you will always be here. With us. With all that breathes and slinks and sucks and shambles in the darkest reaches of our beloved mall, when the lights go out and the shadows grow long and the smell of Bethy's Pretzels permeates your very soul.

Thanks for visiting the mall! If you enjoyed this pamphlet, please consider making a small contribution to the Orford Parish Historical Society. We keep local history alive!

(Donations are not tax deductible.)

Conferring With Ghosts Between the Hours of Three and Four-Forty-Five in the Morning

~ Elou Carroll

There is a sign on the back porch that reads *Everything Will Be Okay Unless It Isn't.* No one questions the validity of the sign, nor its presence, nor the fact that it changes daily—yesterday's message, *Concentrate On What You Can't Control, So You Won't Have To Feel Guilty.* The house with the faded blue picket fence has been empty for nearly fifty years.

Right now, the house is not empty. There is a girl sitting in the middle of the staircase, picking at the frayed edges of a moldy runner. No one saw her enter the house and no one will see her leave. It is three-ten in the morning, the neighborhood is asleep. The neighborhood has work, responsibilities, children to care for.

The girl does not work. The girl is, instead, failing university; she tries to blame her boyfriend, friends, mum, dad, seven-year-old Alsatian but even she does not find this convincing.

She likes to visit abandoned places and wallow in the dust. She does this when she should be sleeping. She doesn't want to be sleeping.

There are rivers of dust flowing down either side of the stairs. The girl traces a question mark and lingers on the dot, presses her finger down until the tip turns white. She asks a question of the stairs and when they do not answer, she kicks the banister. The crunch makes her teeth hurt.

Back at home, her boyfriend is unaware of her absence. In the house with the rotted wooden door, someone is aware of her presence.

"Where do you think she comes from?" they ask.

"Nowhere I know, not with that outfit," someone else responds. "Never seen such a thing."

"Hello?" She's on her feet and the staircase creaks.

"Did you hear that? She speaks!" Someone says.

"Do you think she can hear us? I don't think she can hear us. Not really. They want to hear us but they never usually manage it," someone else is certain.

"I can hear you," she says, "but you're speaking very quietly and I'm not sure where you are."

"'Not sure where we are,' she says. Not sure where we are but she's standing on our staircase." Someone else might huff.

"Blocking the way too!" Someone might be crossing their arms. "No manners."

"Oh," says the girl, "excuse me."

She hops down the steps and into the long hallway. She traces another question in the dust with the toe of her shoe. The girl clasps her hands behind her back and waits, when they do not speak again she looks up and down the hall and wonders if she's imagining things. The girl is prone to fits of imagination and the someones do not contradict her.

When she is at home and her mind is pacing the hallway outside their bedroom, her boyfriend asks her to sit, hold his hands, talk. The girl does not do any of these things.

Instead of standing still, the girl explores the house with the scuffed cream wallpaper. One room in particular is difficult to open. From what she can see, it is full of hundreds and hundreds of rough cardboard signs. Through the gap in the door one board is visible—*It's Not Over. Yet.*—along with half of another. The half message reads: *Remember [...] To Eat [...] A Day.*

The girl considers what a day might taste like, and comes to the conclusion that it would depend entirely on whether it were a Sunday or a Tuesday, a Wednesday or a Friday. She thinks she might like to eat Saturday best, and has decided that it would taste like crisp ice water, freedom and sugar.

The door won't budge. The girl strokes another question into the wood, rests her head on its surface. Thumps once, twice. Sighs.

Someone follows her to the kitchen.

Someone else is already watching the girl disturb their crockery. She opens their cupboards, moves long-forgotten plates and cups, chokes on their dust.

"She's quite rude," someone says.

"Doesn't respect her elders," someone else agrees.

"It's rude to talk about someone as if they're not here, especially if you're not really here yourselves," says the girl.

"Do you think she's lost?" Someone might be pressing a finger to their chin.

Someone else might be doing likewise. "I think she must be."

The girl crosses her arms and decides the someones might leave her alone if she glares hard enough. It works on her boyfriend, who huffs and shuffles off until she comes to find him with her hands in her pockets and her shoulders hunched up by her ears. He opens his arms to her, and she dithers from one foot to the other.

The someones huff too but remain close. She is in their house and they will not be going anywhere; they were inside long before the girl and will linger longer still when she leaves. The girl kicks a cupboard door and it abandons its hinges. She thinks she should apologize.

She doesn't apologize.

While she is standing in the kitchen with her arms crossed and her frown drawn down from her forehead, a square of bent cardboard makes its way from the back porch, past the kitchen, down the hallway, through the house with the faded blue picket fence, rotted wooden door and scuffed cream wallpaper, and slips through the crack in the door to the sign room; someone else is carrying it, but the girl cannot see them and reasons that she must be dreaming.

The girl is pinching herself when a pristine piece of card makes its way in the other direction. Someone carries this one and though she likewise cannot see them, she is sure she is not dreaming. Her bicep bears the tiny crescent moons to prove it.

Arms now unfolded, she peers round the door-frame and squints into the dark. The torch on her keys is dim and useless. Her phone is on her night stand back at home. The house is no longer wired for electricity, though the light switches still tease in their wall sockets. The back door opens and the card slips out, stands up and the door swings shut.

Someone stands next to it.

The girl has never been on the porch because it faces too many windows and she does not want to be accused of delinquency. She does, however, want to see the new sign and so she looks over her shoulder and makes sure there is no one there to see her trespass.

Someone else is at the kitchen window.

Someone joins them.

Both someones eye her dusty footprints on the old wood, see her cross her fingers, crouch down low.

"Do you think she'll read it?" Someone else asks. "I don't think she'll read it."

"She has the eyes for it but she won't take it in." Someone is solemn.

"She really ought to. But she won't."

"Not likely, no," someone agrees.

The girl pictures her bedroom; back at home, her boyfriend might stretch out an arm and brush the negative space in which her body should be sleeping. A frown might shape his eyebrows and he might curl up, shiver, but will not wake. He is a heavy sleeper and he seldom notices her leaving, nor does he stir at her return.

It is four-forty-five in the morning. At the house, there is a sign on the back porch that sometimes reads *Call Your Mother,* othertimes *There's No Use Being Scared Of The Dark, It's The Light You Should Be Worried About,* or *The Other Side Is Almost Exactly The Same As The Side You Came From.* No one questions the validity of the sign, nor its presence—least of all the girl who should be sleeping. Right now, the sign reads *Skin Is More Forgiving Than Dust* and the girl is reading and not reading it at the selfsame time.

Selfies

~ Nina Kiriki Hoffman

I learned to take selfies from Walter, my most recent husband.

When we were out in public, Walter liked to document. He often broke into what we were doing to pose us in front of something or someone fabulous so he could take a selfie. He gloried in putting pictures of us up on his Facebook page to show all the other losers in the world what an amazing life he was leading with his trophy wife.

Yesterday, I went to his Facebook account to look at that gallery of us looking like a celebrity couple leading a fantasy life. I need to delete the account soon; any record of me as Walter's wife must disappear, because I don't get facelifts between my marriages, and I don't want facial recognition software to be able to identify me.

Walter was my best and my worst husband so far: Our two life-lines, the apparent and the real, were both interesting, and I liked him better than I liked my other husbands.

With every husband, I have a line. I put up with a lot from them. Then they cross that line, and I kill them.

Walter crossed the line after we'd been married about three years. He broke my arm. Luckily my right arm, not my dominant left. I still had the strength and skill to kill him and make it look accidental, though I had to wait a couple of weeks after he broke my arm. I wrapped the cast in plastic so it wouldn't get blood on it.

All the death stuff takes a while to settle, if you want to get away with murder. You have to be grief-stricken and do a bunch of acting for the few friends your husband allows you once he really gets into controlling you, and all his so-called friends, too. Husbands I've had are usually charismatic and look like they lead perfect lives, so they have lots of acquaintances. I don't know that I've ever had a husband who had really good friends.

The selfie thing—I liked that. I don't keep souvenirs, because that's one of the easiest things for police to use against you in a court of law. My memories are my treasures. But, I thought, how about pictures of myself while I'm recuperating from being with someone who abused me, and while I'm transforming myself into the next trophy wife? Nobody could convict me of anything based on those.

I went blond after I killed Walter. I experimented with sparkly makeup instead of subtle and classy. I took a ton of selfies in different lighting, trying to decide whether I looked too trashy to attract the kind of man I wanted. Walter was the richest man I'd ever killed. It was nice to have money, but I was ready for a different flavor.

When I studied my selfies, I noticed another person in the pictures, even in the ones I took when I was alone. A shadow man stood behind me.

With the help of the only long-term friend I had, my high school nerd buddy Sully, who knew my whole history and made me fake IDs as necessary, I'd changed my name to Stephanie for this incarnation. As Walter's wife, I had been Margaret. Walter called me Meg at first, and then, as he wore me down, Nutmeg, at least in private. Nutmeg, because I was crazy. He told me my memories were imaginary, and That Didn't Happen. Not easy to convince someone when you have documentation. Sure, he hid all his trophy photos of me after he hit me in a private partition on his computer, but I knew how his mind worked and where he hid his passwords. Also, he left the key to the lock of the basement gallery in a hiding place in the basement, and of course I found that. I took pictures of his pictures and kept an SD card of them in the lining of my purse, just in case.

After I killed Walter, I took a hammer to his laptop and burned his printed-out pictures in our fireplace. I mailed my SD card to Sully and told him not to look, just keep it safe. He's a criminal, but he respects my wishes, or if he doesn't, he never tells me.

I stayed a widow in the house I had shared with Walter for three months, then told anyone who was interested that the house held too many memories. I sold it and moved, as I usually do. I hadn't made any real friends during Nutmeg's life, so I had no regrets.

In my new town, Stephanie joined a gym, took aquarobics and pilates and yoga classes, and buffed up the body I'd let go during my Walter period. Some of the guys in the hot tub hit on Stephanie while she was still fat, which told me I still had it, but they weren't the type of men I was interested in.

Between husbands, I never did feel right. I felt better in some ways, but the lust and excitement and satisfaction were all pretty flat.

I documented Stephanie's adventures in character-building in a series of selfies: Stephanie in all kinds of clothes in department store dressing rooms. I didn't buy many. It took me time and many experiments to settle on a new style every time I started over. I needed my selves to be conventionally attractive, and also interesting, and different from each other. Finding the right quirks took work.

In selfie after selfie as I studied them on my laptop, I saw a shadowy figure behind me, near me, sharing a mirror with me. I knew I had been alone all those times.

The shadow grew darker as I fine-tuned Stephanie. Its outline looked familiar.

At the gym, I took a selfie of me on a treadmill, rocking out to songs on my iPhone. Totally innocent and non-prosecutable. A man stood beside me, even though my gym had separate rooms for the women and men to work out in, and it was hard to stand next to someone on a treadmill. The shadow was darker this time, not at all transparent, and I could make out its face.

It was Walter in all his urbane glory, out of place in a gym in his best dark pinstriped suit (the one I had buried him in), every dark hair in place.

I'd never run into this particular problem before. I mean—ghosts? Who believed? If there were ghosts who could do stuff, wouldn't we be drowning in them? Everybody died sooner or later, not all of them peacefully.

I thought about my previous husbands—Rich, Jason, Hank, and Trevor—all resting in different places around the country.

I sat in my apartment bedroom with the lights lit on my vanity table. I monitored my looks, though I was detached about it. Looks were a tool I used to get what I wanted. I took another selfie while I sat there, and Walter's face showed up over my shoulder, staring at me with a big frown. He looked different from the way he had in the treadmill picture, but I wasn't sure how, except his hair was less shellacked.

What if he was around all the time, watching me, judging?

More fool him.

"What do you even want, Walter?" I asked, looking over my shoulder at nothing. I faced forward again, held up the phone, and aimed the back camera toward my face. He was there, right behind me, wearing a ferocious frown. He frowned even more, came forward, and put his hands around my neck. It looked like he was squeezing, but all I felt was a slight chill.

I shrugged. "You got nothing."

His shoulders rose and fell. Wait, what? He wasn't in his suit anymore. Before I could study on that, he let go of me, pursed his lips, and pointed to my hair, now honey blond with platinum highlights. While I was married to him, it had been auburn with golden highlights.

"What? You don't like it?"

He shook his head.

"Tough shit."

He grimaced. He had never liked to hear me use swear words. Which meant I could easily torture him in the afterlife.

"This is the color for my next husband, not my last husband. I'm going to find somebody with different tastes this time. Maybe a little more down home."

He put his hands around my neck again. I took a selfie. He was there in the picture, looking like he was expending great effort to choke me. His arms were bare, and his muscles were bunched up. I was smiling.

"Look at this. It's so weird!" I showed him the selfie, then realized that without the phone camera active, I couldn't see him, so I didn't know whether he was looking. That was no fun. I emailed the picture to myself, then opened up the laptop to put it on a bigger screen, and switched the phone back to camera mode, aiming it around until I found Walter again. He leaned over beside me and looked at the picture.

"What the hell are you wearing?" I asked. "That's not the suit I buried you in! Are you *shopping* in the afterlife?" How could he be wearing metallic green workout shorts and a pink tank top? So undignified! I'd never seen him wear clothes like that.

He looked hot. His butt, sheathed in shiny green cloth, was so nicely defined I wanted to grab it. I snapped a picture of just his butt, then aimed the camera at his face and captured his nasty grin. He stepped back and posed for me, showing off his muscles, lifting his shirt to reveal washboard abs, doing poses like mustachioed strong men in old circus posters.

I took picture after picture, more interested in him dead than I had been while he was alive. Had he always been this toned? I knew he was strong. I'd felt it. But he wore formal or studiedly casual clothes while we were together, except when we were in bed, and he liked that to be dark time. He loved looking at his handiwork on my body, but never liked me to see him clearly.

I sent all the pictures to my laptop and then looked at Walter with the phone's camera. When had he gotten so . . . solid?

He laughed. I could almost hear it—just the thinnest edge of a sound that used to mean he was going to hit me again, harder.

It worried me.

Then he vanished.

☉

My best friend Sully and I rarely met face to face since I started my career as a serial killer. Our pasts were too tangled with things that might make government people spy on us and listen in on what we said to each other. We liked flying below any radar there was.

This time, though, I arranged to meet him. Sully was rooted in place, part of a crime network in San Francisco, and as Stephanie, I had moved to Palo Alto, not too far from where I grew up. I was ready for some California culture after three-plus years in Chicago.

I met Sully at the public library, in one of the private, glass-walled study rooms.

I hadn't seen him in six years. He was still rangy and tall and looked like he hadn't shaved, or brushed his shaggy brown hair in two weeks. I had never been able to figure out how he maintained just that length of prickly golden stubble. The lines around his eyes and mouth were deeper, and his clothes were more ragged and frayed, but he wore expensive tennis shoes, and he'd changed his chunky black plastic glasses to wire rims that made him look like John Lennon. We hugged. He smelled like barbecue and citrus shampoo and something wild, like sage, and he felt warm and solid.

"Nice work with Walter," he said. Sully always knew where I was, and checked my local newspapers for stories about me and my husbands. He watched for coded requests from me in the personal ads, too. He would have seen the article about Walter's car crash.

"Thanks. Only there's a problem," I said. "Take a look at this." I opened my laptop and showed him a slideshow of my selfies. Not every single one, but a time-lapse of Meg's transformation into Stephanie.

Sully said, after I'd shown him about twenty pictures, "I admit to some fascination with this—I've never seen your in-between stages before—but is there a point, or are you just showing off?"

"Wait. Sorry. I thought I edited this down better. I'll skip ahead." I jumped to the treadmill picture and pointed to Walter's shadow.

"So?"

"It's Walter." I jumped back to a picture of me in a dressing room wearing a ridiculous pink satin sheath dress I'd never buy no matter what I looked like. I enjoyed imagining the kind of person who would buy it, though. Playing dress-up was career practice for me.

I pointed to the faint shadow in the dressing room mirror. "See? He starts showing up here . . ."

"Are you crazy?" Sully asked.

"Only in a controlled way." I flipped back to the treadmill shot, then jumped ahead to a picture of Walter in my vanity table mirror, one where he had his hands wrapped around my throat. His features were visible—the grimace that had terrified me while I was Meg. Stephanie could shrug it off.

Sully took a step back. "Whoa!"

"Didn't hurt," I said. "I couldn't even feel it. But—"

Sully pulled his iPhone out of his pocket and turned on the camera. He looked around the room through his screen. He stopped with the phone aimed over my shoulder.

I got out my own phone and took a look. Walter stood there, sure as shootin', back in his good suit again. He smiled at both of us. He looked a little wavery around the edges, but more real than he had before.

Sully set his phone to record video and aimed it at Walter. "Hey, brother," he said. "What is it you're trying to communicate from beyond the grave?"

Walter gave him the finger.

"Who is this man, Nutmeg?" Walter asked, turning to me. His voice was no louder than a whisper, but I could hear it.

"Nutmeg?" Sully asked, still filming Walter.

"Walter's pet name for me," I said. "Walter, this is Sully, my childhood friend. What are you doing here?"

Walter smiled and buried his hands in his pockets. "I'm a trifle displeased with you, sweetheart. I had no plans to die." He sounded a little louder. His edges had stabilized. Why was he getting more real?

I said, "Neither did I, and the way you were going, it looked like I was headed there. It was you or me, and I chose survival for me."

He frowned.

"So are you haunting me because I killed you?" I asked. "What do I have to do to get rid of you?"

He smiled. "Why would I tell you that?" He turned to Sully, shot him with a finger-gun, then expanded outward, as though he were inflatable and someone was blowing more air into him. His outside edge went right through me, an icy wave. I couldn't stop shuddering; my teeth ached, and my nerves were still firing.

Sully stopped filming. He was shuddering, too; Walter had moved through him as he blew up bigger than the room. Maybe we were still inside his edges.

We put the video on the laptop and watched it. Sully shook his head, stopped, then shook his head again. "I do forgeries and hacking," he said. "I don't do ghosts."

We were sitting at the study-room table with the computer in front of us. I snuck my phone up and took a selfie with me and Sully in it. There was Walter, his face more demonic than human, grinning between me and Sully. He'd grown fangs.

I showed my phone to Sully.

"No," he said. "I love you, Polly, but I can't—I don't—I

got no skills for this." He grabbed his battered briefcase and his phone and left the room.

I sat back, feeling cold and alone. Sully had always been there for me, no matter what I did. I couldn't believe he would leave me now.

But the door had closed behind him. I waited, and he didn't come back.

I swallowed. I took a few deep breaths. I figured out my next move. Sully had already helped me set up my Stephanie identity, and I'd gotten her look down now. I flipped up the laptop lid to go online.

"Hey," Walter whispered in my ear. "I've met some interesting people over here. Look behind me."

I could hear Walter, even though I wasn't looking at him. I sighed and aimed my phone toward his voice. He was there, looking spiffy and charismatic again. Other shadows hovered behind him. I snapped a picture. They were still just stains on the air, not solid like Walter, but I suspected if I could see them clearly, they'd look a lot like Rich, Jason, Hank, and Trevor.

"We've had some lovely talks," Walter whispered.

I turned off my phone. Maybe ostrich mode would work for me: he couldn't bother me if I didn't look at him. I plugged in the laptop, went online, and started a new Match.com account. I needed a selfie. I looked at my most recent ones. They all had Walter in them. Well, I could edit him out. I chose one of the ones I had taken at my vanity table and cropped and blackened Walter's image out of the picture, then posted it and set up my subscription using the new credit card Sully had gotten for Stephanie Farrell. I registered with the nickname Steffy and said I liked homemaking and entertaining.

The website showed me singles near me, and I studied their pictures, wondering who they really were. It took me a lot of dates with a lot of people to find my husbands. I didn't want to marry anyone who didn't deserve me.

I heard breathing in my ear. "I like Mr. TakeAChance," Walter whispered. I turned toward his voice, then remembered I was ignoring him. Still, I looked hard at Mr. TakeAChance, and ended up sending him a message.

⊙

The next time I took a selfie, again while sitting at the vanity table in the bedroom, Walter was back beside me, looking into the phone's camera and smiling. This time he was wearing a joke nightshirt I had bought him for our first Christmas together, flannel with little Grinches all over it. He'd never worn it while he was alive. He'd been angry and disgusted when he opened it, and I spent the rest of Christmas in bed with a lot of bruises.

"You burned that. How'd you get it back?" I asked.

He smiled and waggled his eyebrows. Had he grown a sense of humor since he died?

He pointed at the phone. "Take another picture," he whispered. "I'll make a face."

He'd never been playful. I shrugged and took a picture, and then another, and another. In each he was doing a different expression. He even pushed up his nose into a pig snout, and did fish lips. If he'd been this fun while he was alive, maybe I wouldn't have killed him.

At last he leaned forward and licked my ear while I took a picture, and I felt it. I felt it. He left a trace of slimy wetness on me.

I shuddered and turned the phone off.

I could still see him. A faint, shadowy image on the air, but still there.

I ran out of my bedroom and into the kitchen. His stain didn't follow me. I grabbed my coat and purse and went out. I went to Green Park and walked off my shudders, then went home, to find my phone had run out of charge. When I plugged it in again, it notified me it had no more storage space.

Somehow Walter had managed to use it to take more selfies. Hundreds of them. I deleted and deleted, and there were still more.

A knock sounded behind me, and I turned to see Walter at my open bedroom door. He looked real. "Hey, baby," he said. "You know how pictures steal a little of your soul? It works the other way if you're dead already. Welcome me back?"

☉

I still take selfies. I've noticed a slow leak of what makes me myself slipping away, a tiny increment gone with each picture I take. I'm not sure where I'm going. I just know I don't want to stay here anymore.

ACE of PENTACLES.

Vieux Carré

~ Rebecca Ruvinsky

I didn't expect to find him at a bar. It had been a long time since I had seen him last, but as soon as my eyes fell upon him, my heart stilled first in instant recognition—then quickened.

He was ready behind the counter when I approached the bar and slid into an open seat. I watched him work, mixing and shaking and stirring drinks together, expertly and elegantly carrying out his craft. He moved without hesitation, always reaching for the next bottle, always knowing where it was. He kept his eyes down, completely focused, yet I could still sense his attention on me.

When he slid me a drink, he finally met my gaze.

"Blue eyes this time?" I said as I lifted the glass to my lips. Calling them blue couldn't capture the true depth of color. They reminded me of the color of the sky from when I had learned of my mother's death—no, the color of the ocean from when my sister was lost among the waves—no, the color of the lie my husband had been wearing when he had—

Ah. He was already getting into my head. I lowered my eyes, taking a sip from my drink.

"I think they flatter me," he answered, his hands still in motion even as he stood in front of me. I let my gaze wander over his body. He had aged with grace, as attractive as the last time I had seen him, tall and slim with high cheekbones and long, beautiful fingers. His bartender's uniform, sleek black against his pale skin, fit him like a well-tailored suit.

"Quite so, but let me handle the flattery," I murmured, sipping at my drink again.

His lips twitched into a slight smile. "As long as I can return the favor."

It was impossible to look away from him, a controlled chaos in the making of drinks, his hands moving hypnotically, with confidence in every gesture.

He finished up a martini with a twirl of lemon before sliding it over to someone else at the bar, who turned away too swiftly for me to see their face. "How's the drink?" he asked, drawing my attention back.

I'd never had a better one, but I just shrugged. "It's good. Strong and smooth. What is it?"

"Vieux Carré." He started shaking up another drink. "It comes from New Orleans. Have you ever been?"

I took another slow sip of my cocktail before answering. "No, I haven't. Perhaps I'll book a ticket for tomorrow. Top one-hundred places to visit before you die, or so they say."

He tipped his head down slightly, so I could see his smile without even lifting my eyes. "Tomorrow? A lot could happen between tonight and tomorrow."

"Like someone poisoning my drink?" I asked dryly, lifting it in a toast to him before downing what was left.

He whisked the empty glass away as soon as it touched the counter, ever the vigilant bartender. "Nothing so gauche as that."

"Then if I live through the night, you'll know where to find me next." As if poison would affect me by now.

"Oh, I'm always keeping my eye on you." He began pouring bottles into a mixing glass. A dash of bitters swirled into ice and a haze of amber liquids, all twirled together with deft hands. "You go to so many fascinating places."

"What can I say? I have a long bucket list to check off."

The drink was strained into a short glass, then topped with a cherry. He slid it to me. "How long could it be?"

"A million and one experiences, of course. And as you so kindly pointed out," I ran my finger around the rim of my new glass, "no time like the present."

"Then where am I on that list?" he asked, his voice dropping down to a purr.

I couldn't help the grin, but disguised it by tossing down the drink—just as good as the first time. "Not to fret. I'm saving you for last."

"That's what they all say, but," he leaned forward, resting his elbows on the counter, "most never have that choice. You shouldn't, either. How do you do it?"

"You must enjoy chasing me as much as I enjoy being chased." His proximity made me feel more alive than ever. I knew he was looking right at me. Sweet adrenaline flooded my veins, more intoxicating than the drinks, and I fought the impulse to run my tongue over my lips.

He pulled away. "Every chase must end eventually."

"I'm more for enjoying the journey rather than the destination." I drew in a slow, sweet breath of air. "And if you could catch me, you would have."

He turned a glass around in his hands, looking down at it. Relief and disappointment mingled at his eyes turning away from me. "Well, that's the interesting part, isn't it?" he murmured. "I've followed you for so far, and so long, and yet you're still sitting here."

"And yet I'm still sitting here," I echoed in a whisper. I couldn't see the expression on his face, but he stepped away, and I let my attention wander away from him, leaning back against my barstool to look around.

It was a classier place than I normally went to, all blacks and golds and greys with soft, dim lighting throughout. It was comfortable while still looking exclusive, fancy in a way that was completely effortless. People were all around, filling up the tables and booths and barstools, but it didn't feel crowded—or loud, for that matter, only a general murmur of conversation reaching my ears. And the people themselves . . . They were all strangers, their faces indistinct, hazy in the lighting, almost blurry . . .

The sound of ripping paper drew my attention back to the bar. He was back, placing a receipt in front of me, and as I reached for it, our fingertips grazed. His skin was cool to the touch, yet my pulse raced. I wanted to kiss him, see if his lips were as cold as his hands, yet I couldn't even look into his eyes.

Instead, I looked at the receipt as he returned to mixing his drinks. It was a long list, longer than my two drinks, and handwritten in a quick scrawl. I trailed my fingers over the letters.

Instead of drinks, there were deaths. Instead of prices, there were dates.

So, so many.

My hands trembled as I read it.

Car crash, 03/12. Mugging, 05/22. Stairs, 02/07. Flu, 08/10. Car crash, 10/14. Choking, 09/13.

The list went on and on.

"Such a ripe soul. So many beautiful deaths I had planned for you," he said. He was right in front of me, cleaning a glass, but I couldn't bring myself to see if he was smiling or not. I knew him. I saw him in the reflection of the glassy eyes of those I had loved, saw him while my soul longed for him, because my soul was done growing and was ready to go home, wanting to be plucked from my body by his long, pale fingers . . .

I set the receipt on the counter, hiding my hands in my lap. "What can I say? I love a challenge."

"Ah, for the both of us, and what a challenge you are. You have escaped all of my attempts, outstepped me at every turn. I try, but it never changes a thing."

"What? Still pretending that you actually want to catch me?" I teased. My heart pounded in my ears, fear drowned out by exhilaration.

He rested his hands on the countertop, and I found I preferred the motion to this stillness. Since I didn't want to look at his eyes, I found myself staring at his lips. I wondered how close love and death were intertwined, wondered if his lips were salty, wondered if he was made from the salt of everyone's tears.

"I know you," he said. "I know the experiences resting within you, waiting to be released. Love and grief, laughter and loss, and all the moments in-between. I know how you've cried, whether from sorrow or sheer happiness, and thought of me. I know your soul is ready, that you have lived all you were meant to live. So how are you still here, resisting me?" His voice was calm and soft. He had always had a mild smile and gentle eyes, I remembered; he was made of patience.

There was no loving him, but there was longing. I wanted to look into his eyes again, get lost in that wide blue sky. That sky—those waves—his tie—now all contained in a glance, in his eyes. I wondered what color his eyes would be if I looked up now.

"I thought you had taken enough from me." My smile was colored with all the memories of a life that was now long behind me, but never in the past. "No, not thought. I decided you had taken enough from me, and I learned that there is life in defiance. I refused to be taken."

I sensed him looking me over again, a careful and deliberate scrutiny that narrowed me down to bones, blood, and a beating heart. Goosebumps prickled my skin.

"Defiance that can sustain a life would overtake all else there is," he said.

"How would you know?" I lifted my head to match his

stare, baring my neck. He studied me with gentle grey eyes, almost absent of color. His smile was sad and mild, and he was so still. I continued, quiet and sure, "You've never looked death in the face and refused to be whisked away."

He huffed out a breath that may have been a chuckle, but didn't pull his eyes away from mine. Was he as entranced by me as I was by him?

"Even you cannot live forever."

"It's not about trying to live. It's about making sure not to die. I know how I would miss that thrill." I paused, holding his gaze. "As I'm sure you would, too."

He dropped his eyes from mine first, reaching forward to take the receipt. I surprised myself by putting a hand over the back of his, and he met my eyes again.

Blue like unshed tears, like gentle waves, like seeing the sky for the first time in a week.

I lifted my hand from his, then rose from my chair. "Thanks for the drink."

"I'll put it on your tab," he said, and whisked the receipt away.

Seahorses and Other Gifts

~ *Tristan Morris*

A gift.

Or, a gift is what it was called, anyway. Surely it had many characteristics of a kindness. It was grown out of love, carved with delicate care, animated not by casual thought, but by a great deal of the giver's money, time and blood. Much was sacrificed to bring it into being, without any intention that it should benefit the maker. It came in wrapping paper, with a little bow on top. The paper had seahorses on it.

And yet, Sarah hated seahorses. So many of the things she received had seahorses on them—objects soon assimilated into her monument, her shrine to that which was unwanted but could not be thrown away. The closet she dreaded to open but would never empty. The closet that did not contain anything she would consider a gift.

She tore the wrapping paper. Within it was a small wooden box; hardwood, square, brass hinges. A seahorse was carved onto the lid. It very much resembled a ring box, but when she opened it, there was nothing inside, not even the felt coverings within which a ring might potentially be placed.

Momentarily confused, she shut it again, wondering if perhaps something was supposed to be within and the container had been packed incorrectly. But before she could examine it any further, the box spoke.

"This evening, your space heater sets your bedsheets on fire, and you burn to death."

☉

The box spoke many times as the days passed. It was, to Sarah, an embarrassment, a shame, something to be hidden out of politeness, like breaking wind or her remarkably nasal laugh. Whenever she felt the box tremble, felt its lid twitch, she would rise and excuse herself from the room, feigning some biological urge or claiming her phone was ringing. Then, when she was hidden in the bathroom or an empty section of hallway, she would let it speak.

"Today's the day your boss finally fires you."

"The janitor is planning to steal your purse out of your desk drawer when you're at lunch."

"That sniffle this morning was pneumonia."

Of course, her deception could only last so long. She was sitting at her desk when the truth came out, discussing the results of her employer's diversity program with the HR manager from up the hall. He had asked her for some numbers, and she had clicked through her laptop until she found them. "Overall it's good news," she was saying, "but employee confidence is still low, even when—"

"This afternoon, he tells the entire HR team you're a bitch," her box said.

She'd left it on her desk. They both turned the source of the noise, to the little wooden box with the seahorse on the cover. His expression was quizzical, hers stricken, but fate did her a small kindness, and he spoke first.

"Oh, that's one of those, uh . . ." He waved generally in its direction. "Evil box things. Right?"

"It's a Safety Box," Sarah said. "It predicts bad things that might happen to you today. Literally today. Warns you of anything that might happen before midnight."

"Well, it's not very accurate." He flashed her a smile. "You're good at your job. And pleasant, if that matters. Sorry, I know expecting women to always be pleasant is sexist in-and-of itself, but, you are."

"No. I know. It's actually quite inaccurate," she said. "It makes exactly one-hundred predictions a day, but only one of them is correct."

"You're going to die in a plane crash," the box said.

"See?" she continued, gesturing at it. "I'm not getting on a plane today. So unless a plane falls out of the sky and lands on the office, I'm pretty sure that one isn't true."

The man from HR frowned. "If it makes a hundred predictions a day, and only one of them is correct, then . . ." He made a vague gesture in the air. "Sorry, I just don't see why you'd buy this? I know they've been in the news a lot recently, and are like, trendy or whatever, but it doesn't seem that useful."

"It was a gift. From my parents."

"Oh," said the man from HR. A long pause hung in the air, perhaps as he wondered why she did not simply throw it away. But if such thoughts were on his mind, he did not voice them. "That must be frustrating."

"It's fine," Sarah waved him off. "Like I said, not going to die in a plane crash today. It's embarrassing and annoying but that's about it. All I need to do is ignore whatever it says."

"Sure," he said. "Anyway, you were saying about employee confidence?"

After he left, the box said, "Your analysis was wrong, and he'll realize it this afternoon."

As she packed up her things at the end of the day, the box said, "You've forgotten something important, and it will be gone when you get back tomorrow."

As she waved goodbye to the security guard at the front desk, and walked out into the parking lot, the box said, "You're going to be hit by a car."

She ignored it, of course.

She was not three steps out of the building when Steve from Accounting ran her down with his Toyota. He'd been texting while driving.

⊙

When Sarah regained consciousness, she was in a hospital, her limbs in casts, her head in a brace. The sheets were stained with blood; her blood. The little box sat beside her bed, and it said: "Your injuries are fatal. You will die today."

With a raspy voice, she asked the doctors how long she had, but they told her she would pull through. Then the box said, "The hospital bill will be enormous. You'll be in debt for the rest of your life."

But she spoke with the nurses, and they informed her her insurance covered everything. Then the box said, "Your parents are going to visit, and they'll spend an hour talking about how much you loved seahorses when you were twelve."

It said a few other things, but Sarah was scarcely listening. She already knew which prediction was coming true.

☉

When she got out of the hospital, Sarah's coworkers threw her a party. They told her how glad they were that she was well, and offered her gifts and gentle hugs. She felt liked, and appreciated, and the company cut her a sizable check in return for her agreement not to sue. Then, her boss suggested they all go out to lunch. It was a pretty good welcome.

While her entire team tried to crowd in around one table at the restaurant, the box shook in Sarah's pocket. When she withdrew it, and held it up to her ear, it whispered so quietly that nobody else could hear: "You're going to get food poisoning from the burgers."

From her purse, she withdrew a tiny spiral-bound notebook and pencil. The front page of the notebook had three columns drawn in it, each labeled in her tiny, immaculate handwriting: *Absurd, Plausible, Likely.*

Absurd already had two entries from that morning: that she was going to be abducted by aliens, and that she was going to be murdered by communists. *Likely* had only one entry, that her welcome-back party was going to suck. So, she crossed out "Welcome Back Party Sucks," as it was evidently not true, and underneath *Plausible* filled in, "Food poisoning from burgers."

Then, she updated the tally at the bottom of the page. 4/100 so far that day.

"Actually," she said, as she put the notebook away. "I know this place has great burgers, but could I get the salad instead? I'm feeling like something light."

None of her coworkers got sick, so that one was evidently incorrect as well, but the salad was good and so the effort had cost her little. Over the course of the day, she continued to update her little notebook, both the entries and the tally.

The tally was key. The tally told her the collective probability that the true event of the day was already written in her notebook. At one hundred predictions for the day, she could be certain that one of the fears on her list was valid. By extension, at one hundred predictions, it was possible to be safe. The lower the count, the lower her certainty.

For example, prediction forty-seven for the day was, "Your cast is going to slip on the bathroom tisle, and you'll hit your head on the sink and die." Such a danger was easily negated—she used the porta-potty at the construction site across the street and then washed her hands in the employee kitchen—but she couldn't even claim 50/50 odds that that warning was the right one.

By contrast, as she was packing up for the day, prediction eighty-nine was, "Traffic on the drive home will be horrible." Such a prediction not only merited an entry in the *Likely* column, but as a late-day *Likely*, had more than a 50% chance of being true. More than a 50% chance that a little traffic would be the worst thing to happen to her that day.

It was a comforting thought. So comforting that when traffic did indeed turn out to be horrible, Sarah found a great smile playing across her face. She made it home alive, and cheerfully ignored predictions ninety, ninety-one, ninety-two, ninety-three, ninety-four, ninety-five, ninety-six, ninety-seven, ninety-eight, and ninety-nine.

As she turned off her apartment lights to go to sleep, the thought occurred to her that she had only ninety-nine tallies in her little notebook. But, she imagined that she must have forgotten to record an entry, and thought nothing of it.

At 11:59 PM exactly, the box woke her.

"Today," it said, "two predictions come true."

☉

But did they? Is "Two predictions come true" itself a prediction? And if so, is it true? Or, is "two predictions come true" false, because only one predicted event actually happened? It was a logic puzzle, of the sort Sarah hated in school.

Except in school, the penalty for getting the answer wrong wasn't potentially death.

At midnight, she got out of bed and spent an hour googling the problem on her laptop. When that failed to produce a definitive answer, she ordered textbooks off the internet, guides to logic and math, PDFs for instant delivery. She had detested such books when she was a student and certainly didn't want to read them as a free adult, but the alternative was too dangerous. All night she read them, and when she wasn't able to finish her reading by the time she had to leave for work, she called in sick, claiming her leg needed to be looked at.

Her box spoke twelve times over the course of the morning. In her notebook, she made eight entries in the *Absurd* column (mostly relating to dying in spectacular ways), three entries in the *Plausible* column (mostly relating to her friends secretly hating her), and one entry in the *Likely* column.

"Your research is wrong; you have no idea what you're doing."

But she'd expected that, and after an entire night and morning reading *An Introduction to Logic Puzzles* and *The Basics of Set Theory*, she was fairly certain she knew the answer, that "two predictions come true," was not a valid prediction and was therefore false. The box was only messing with her.

Probably.

"If you don't get something done today," the box said, "your coworkers will think you're lazy." That was prediction thirteen for the day, *Plausible*. But when she pulled out her laptop, it said, "If you get too much done today, they'll know you faked calling in sick." Prediction fourteen, also *Plausible*.

It took her nearly an hour to decide how to avoid both dangers: she would get exactly two-and-a-half hours of work done, and send several emails apologizing for being behind due to her injury. That way, people would see her working and know she was industrious, but nobody would question that she didn't put in a full day. She was quite proud of that plan.

Plus, it gave her plenty of time to deal with other dangers, like prediction twenty-nine, "The food truck up the street has contaminated meat," and prediction forty-four, "You're going to be mugged on the way to the grocery store." She paid extra to have groceries delivered, and spent all afternoon cooking for herself.

Later, prediction thirty-seven came true: "You will feel a brief but intense sadness regarding Mr. Scruffles."

Mr. Scruffles, her cat, had died when she was fourteen. So it wasn't the worst thing that could have happened to her in a day.

☉

"Your productivity will suffer due to stress," her box predicted. But that one wasn't true. Quite the opposite.

Every warning that her coworkers doubted her competence made her double and triple-check her work. Every prediction that her skills were beginning to atrophy drove her to study in her spare time. Every tally in a notebook that foretold of a coworker who secretly despised her heralded the birth of a new friendship. She went so out of her way to be nice to the people who might otherwise plot against her.

People joked that the crash must have knocked the fluff out of her head. She was always so prepared, so focused, so *there* in the moment, with a clarity that only adrenaline could provide.

And her newfound focus was not restricted to the office. The box with the seahorse on the top helped her in all sorts of ways. She was eating healthier, being aware of the sheer number of takeout places with tainted food or staff that wanted her dead. She was exercising more, given the number of acquaintances who could potentially whisper that she was fat and lazy. And she almost never got sick, due to a three part plan of scrupulously avoiding all germs, being up to date on all her inoculations, and turning up at her doctor's office roughly once every-other week.

Felix even asked her out. Felix, the cute guy from IT. He was tall, handsome, charming, well-educated, and from what everyone said, crushing on her.

"He roofies your drink," her box said, prediction ninety-seven for the day.

Ninety-seven was too high. Much too high. No other predictions had come true yet that day. Possibly because she avoided them, but possibly because Felix was a rapist, and she could hardly take that chance. So she canceled their date, and didn't return his calls after that. It was safer that way.

But, she was still happy he asked her out. Cute guys didn't usually give her the time of day. Maybe, she thought, all the exercise was working for her. It was good.

"Do you like the Safety Box?" her parents asked, calling her a week after her cast finally came off.

"It's great," she said, "I love it. Really helped me get my life in order."

Then her hand started to shake, and she didn't know why, a tremble that started in her fingertips and worked its way up to her wrist, her arm. Like she was shivering.

"I'm so glad," her father said. "I carved the top myself. You *loved* seahorses so much when you were little."

"That shaking is the onset of a seizure," the box said. "You're having a stroke."

"I gotta go," Sarah said, hanging up the phone. She immediately called 911, and had an ambulance sent to her house. As she waited for them to arrive, she pulled out her notebook, and added the prediction to her log.

It went under *Plausible*. People in their twenties rarely had seizures, but it could happen.

⊙

Her insurance had very little sympathy for her calling an ambulance because she had a shiver. They declined to pay for any of it, and the hospital was cruel. Including her CAT scan for possible stroke, the bill came to over $25,000.

But she had the money the company had given her from the car crash. So it was fine. She didn't panic, or scream, or rant. She paid the bill, and then looked for an insurance plan that *would* cover her in every eventuality.

Such a plan was, of course, much more expensive than her current one, but that was fine; she didn't need to eat out or go to the movies or fritter away her money on other things. Frugality was key. And, she needed to be closer to the hospital in case something happened, and in a low-crime area, and somewhere she could add extra locks to her doors in case of home invasion.

So she left her comfortable three-bedroom in the downtown, and moved to a studio apartment near the hospital. It was much cheaper. The difference paid for extra insurance, extra security, extra peace of mind, and when the box whispered, "This place is full of lead-based paint." She took the time to test every wall herself.

The test for lead came back negative. She repainted the walls anyway.

Her shivering got worse, and a dozen trips to the hospital in a dozen days did not reveal the cause. She shook when nobody was around, and when others were around, she locked her eyes on them like a frightened animal. She tried meditation, medication, mindfulness, until she was reminded that meditation was bullshit, medication could poison her, and she was already pretty damn mindful.

She was more mindful than most, she thought. She saw to every detail of her life.

Of course, driving to work presented its own problems: carjackers, mass shootings, muggings, car accidents, natural disasters. Her company's office was quite old. What if it wasn't up to code, and there was an earthquake? It could collapse and kill her. She looked up the office with the County Registrar, and all its inspections did appear up to date, but those forms were so easy to fake.

"Today you will be exposed to asbestos due to your employer faking a safety inspection of the office." Prediction eighty-seven, *Likely*.

She didn't blunder into her boss's office, shouting that she had to work from home or she'd die. "Your coworkers will become convinced you've gone crazy," was prediction twelve that day, and a prediction several days before that. No; she planned, she prepared. She invented a story about caring for an elderly relative, with tragic implications and reasonable supporting evidence. She assembled an unimpeachable case that working from home would improve both her life and her job performance.

"Well," her boss said, "normally I'd say no, but you are one of our best employees. So as long as your productivity doesn't drop, I suppose it's okay."

Months of hard work paid off in that moment. She said her goodbyes, left the office for the last time, and returned to her apartment. Her apartment in one of the safest buildings in the city, where all possible toxic chemicals had been identified and removed, where there were a dozen locks on the door. Two months worth of food was in storage in case of natural disaster, along with several safety kits. She had her work laptop for talking with her coworkers, and for talking with everyone else, a burner phone and a high-security machine, devices that ensured no criminal on the internet could identify her real location or steal her banking information.

The day she came home, her box said, "You're going to be hit by a car," and with a smile, she wrote it under *Absurd.*

She slept soundly that night, for the first time in so long.

The next morning, her box said, "Today, the world comes to an end." She started a new page in her notebook, added her three columns, and under *Absurd* wrote "Apocalypse." Then she made a tally at the bottom, *1/100,* and got up to start the day. She had to check for spiders, check for mold, check for spoiled food, eat a perfectly balanced breakfast, and start work an hour early before anyone could think ill of her for working from home.

She was examining her bananas when the box said, "Today, the world comes to an end."

It was the first time she had ever heard the box make the same prediction twice. Hesitantly, she made another tally in her notebook, but overall thought it a good thing. "Right," she said aloud, "but only one prediction comes true. So if you predict the same thing twice, that prediction must be wrong."

In reply, the box made its third prediction for the day. "Today, the world comes to an end."

Sarah's shaking returned. She sat at her table, fingers trembling, and waited for the box to tell her she was having a seizure, or had diabetes, or needed to rush to the hospital.

"Today, the world comes to an end."

She hyperventilated, clutching her face, breathing in her hands, whispering profanities to herself over and over. Opening all the locks on her door revealed the building hallway, and she threw a wad of cash halfway through the open doorframe, so it would be visible to anyone passing by. Money, a nice apartment, an un-locked door. She waited for the box to tell her she was going to be robbed.

"Today, the world comes to an end."

She did not go to work. She did not exercise or cook or do any of the other things she meant to do. She spent the whole day researching ways the world could potentially come to an end before midnight that night. Predictions the box made were not predestined. Perhaps she could avert what was to come.

Her conclusions did not inspire her: asteroid impact, nuclear war, a black hole passing through the solar system, supervolcano eruption. None of the ways the world might abruptly end seemed within her power to change.

But didn't she have to try?

She called NASA, and when their general helpline blew her off, she put her considerable research skills to use finding the personal cellphone number of a mid-level director. He picked up his phone, and she argued and screamed and ranted about imminent danger from the stars. But he called her crazy, and hung up.

Two more NASA staff blocked her calls, and by mid-afternoon, she couldn't find any more numbers. That left two possibilities she could theoretically do something about: nuclear war, and a supervolcano.

She couldn't find any numbers for anyone at the DoD—not surprising, really—but a nuclear war wouldn't be instant death for everyone on the planet. Remote areas would survive. Likewise, a supervolcano would not be instantly fatal for the entire population, and she might ride it out if she was lucky and had enough food.

"Today, the world comes to an end."

By four o'clock, it was up to prediction fifty-two, all of them the same. Her car tore out of the parking lot for her apartment, headed first to the bank, then to the nearest shopping center. The car she filled with food, clean water, iodine tablets, filter masks, bullets, a gun, and everything else she thought she might need to survive the apocalypse. Stuffed into the glove compartment was a printout from her research.

Likely targets of nuclear strikes, supervolcanos in the western hemisphere, safest places to ride out the above. She'd found a farmhouse in the middle of nowhere, that was somehow listed on AirBnB.

"Today, the world comes to an end."

She drove all night across the country, watching the clock tick by, the box with the seahorse on the top resting on her dashboard.

"Today, the world comes to an end."

When she found the farmhouse, navigating by GPS, she drove through the picket fence that surrounded it. Perhaps because it was hard to see, or perhaps because she simply didn't see it. Either way, she didn't care. It was too close to midnight.

"Today, the world comes to an end."

She threw all her supplies into the basement, and took shelter under the strongest part of the structure.

"Today, the world comes to an end."

Her hands shook uncontrollably, and it was only with considerable effort that she took out her notebook and little pencil, and made another entry on the tally. When she finally came to rest in the farmhouse, she was up to ninety-one.

With the notebook to her right, the light of her cell-phone to her left, she watched both the tally and the time advance. To her, the room felt as a furnace, and she broke out in a hot sweat. Drops ran down her face and fell from her nose, staining the paper.

Prediction ninety-two came at 11:12 PM. Still the same. Ninety-three came at 11:22, and so forth. Ninety-nine came at 11:59 PM. "Today, the world comes to an end."

One prediction left. One which had to come true.

Her phone didn't display seconds, so she counted them down aloud: sixty, fifty-nine, fifty-eight, and so forth. Tears ran down her face, and her vision blurred as she began to sob. The trembling in her hands was so violent that she clawed at her own flesh, digging long and bloody scratches down her arms.

Then the last prediction came, at the very stroke of midnight.

"Today's the day you finally snap."

CONTRIBUTORS

Michael Barsa

Michael Barsa grew up in a German-Syrian household in New Jersey and spoke no English until he went to school. So began an epic struggle to master the American "R" and a lifelong fascination with language. He now teaches environmental and natural resources law, and his scholarly articles have appeared in several major law reviews, *The Chicago Tribune*, and *The Chicago Sun-Times*.

His first novel, *The Garden of Blue Roses* (released through Underland Press), made the Preliminary Ballot for the Bram Stoker Award for First Novel and received praise from Alice Sebold, Paul Tremblay, *Kirkus Reviews*, and *Library Journal*.

Elou Carroll

Elou Carroll is a graphic designer and freelance photographer who writes. Her work appears or is forthcoming in *Aloe, Emerge Literary Journal, 101 Words, Apparition Lit, Walled Women,* and *perhappened* mag. She is the editor-in-chief of *Crow & Cross Keys*, and she spends far too much time on Twitter (@keychild).

David Hewitt

David A. Hewitt was born in Germany, grew up near Chicago, and spent eight years in Japan, where he studied classical

Japanese martial arts and grew up some more. A graduate of the University of Southern Maine's Stonecoast MFA program in Popular Fiction, he currently teaches English at the Community College of Baltimore County, but has at various times worked as a Japanese translator, an instructor of martial arts, a cabinetmaker's assistant, a pizza/subs/beer delivery guy, and a pet shop boy.

His hobbies include skiing, writing, meditation, writing, disc golf, travel, and writing.

His short fiction has appeared in *Kaleidotrope, Metaphorosis,* and *Mithila Review*; his novelette "The Great Wall of America" is also available from Mithila Press as a standalone book. As a translator of Japanese, his credits include the anime series *Gilgamesh, Kingdom,* and *Kochoki: Young Nobunaga.*

Nina Kiriki Hoffman

Over the past four decades, Nina Kiriki Hoffman has sold adult and young adult novels and more than 350 short stories. Her works have been finalists for the World Fantasy, Mythopoeic, Sturgeon, Philip K. Dick, and Endeavour awards. Her novel *The Thread that Binds the Bones* won a Horror Writers Association Stoker Award, and her short story "Trophy Wives" won a Science Fiction & Fantasy Writers of America Nebula Award.

Nina does production work for the *The Magazine of Fantasy & Science Fiction.* She teaches short story classes through Lane Community College, Wordcrafters in Eugene, and Fairfield County Writers' Studio. She lives in Eugene, Oregon.

For a list of Nina's publications, check out: http://ofearna.us/books/hoffman.html.

Jessie Kwak

Jessie Kwak has always lived in imaginary lands, from Arrakis and Ankh-Morpork to Earthsea, Tatooine, and now Portland, Oregon. As a writer, she sends readers on their own journeys to immersive worlds filled with fascinating characters, gunfights, explosions, and dinner parties. She is the author of supernatural thriller *From Earth and Bone*, the Bulari Saga series of gangster sci-fi novels, and productivity guide *From Chaos to Creativity*.

You can learn more about her at www.jessiekwak.com, or follow her on Twitter (@jkwak).

Tristan Morris

Tristan Morris has authored or co-authored four books, but "Seahorses and Other Gifts" is his first publication in *Underland Arcana*. He organizes the Quills and Sofas writing society, a creative writing association based in the San Francisco Bay area, where he lives with his wife.

Stephen O'Donnell

Stephen O'Donnell is a writer, living in Dublin, Ireland. His short stories have appeared most recently in *Strange Horizons, Short Edition,* and *Typehouse.*

His website is: http://bit.ly/stizzle0dizzle

Jonathan Raab

Jonathan Raab is the author of numerous short stories, veteran advocacy essays, and novels including *Camp Ghoul Mountain Part VI: The Official Novelization* and *The Hillbilly Moonshine Massacre*. He is the editor of several anthologies from Muzzle-land Press, including *Behold the Undead of Dracula: Lurid Tales of Cinematic Gothic Horror* and *Terror in 16-bits.* He lives in Colorado with his wife Jess, their son, and a dog named Egon.

You can find him on Twitter @jonathanraab1.

Rebecca Ruvinsky

Rebecca Ruvinsky is a student, poet, and emerging writer in Orlando, Florida. She has kept a streak of writing a poem every day since 2016, with work published or forthcoming in *Wizards in Space, Prospectus Literary, Sylvia Magazine, From the Farther Trees,* and others. She loves watching rocket launches, reading late into the night, and finding the magical in the mundane.

She can be found on Twitter @writeruvinsky.

PAMELA COLMAN SMITH

The tarot images in this issue of Arcana are from the deck illustrated by Pamela Colman Smith. It was released in 1909 as the Rider-Waite deck (so named, at that time, in reference to its publisher, William Rider & Son). It remains the most influential and widely used tarot deck. While the impetus for the deck came from Arthur Edward Waite, Colman Smith was responsible for the iconography of the cards.

Pamela Colman Smith also illustrated over twenty books, wrote two collections of Jamaican folklore, edited two magazines, and ran the Green Sheaf Press, a small press devoted to women writers. She continued to write and illustrate throughout her life.

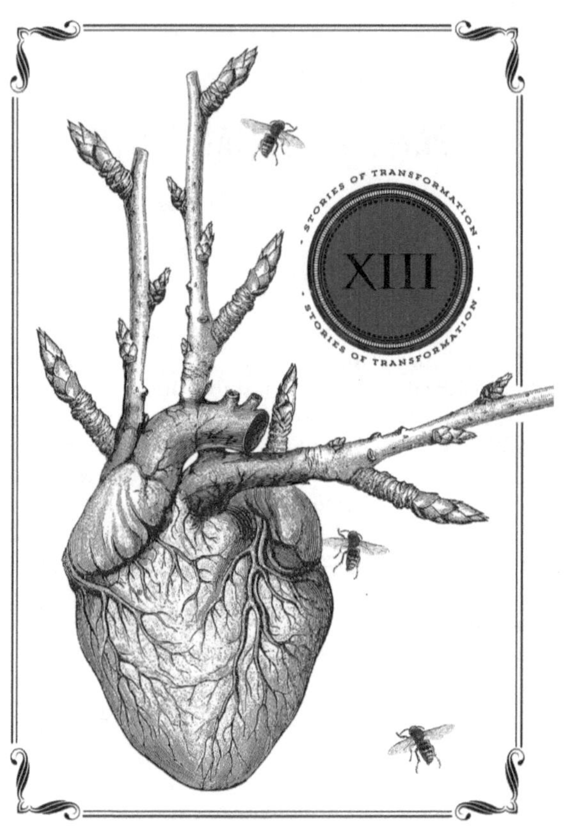

STORIES OF TRANSFORMATION
XIII
STORIES OF TRANSFORMATION

XIII

The thirteenth Tarot card is Death, and he is a symbol not of the end, but of transformation and rebirth. This is the genesis and root of *Thirteen: Stories of Transformation*. The twenty-eight authors of this collection are voices—new and old—who are not afraid to explore what comes next. Whether it be a life after death, a life without love, a life filled with hunger, or the life shared by a ghost. These are stories of the weird, the mythic, the fantastic, the futuristic, the supernatural, and the horrific.

With stories by Liz Argall • M. David Blake • Richard Bowes • George Cotronis • Amanda C. Davis • Julie C. Day • Jetse de Vries • Jennifer Giesbrecht • Daryl Gregory • Rik Hoskin • Rebecca Kuder • Claude Lalumière • Marc Levinthal • Grá Linnaea • Alex Dally MacFarlane • Juli Mallett • Lyn McConchie • Fiona Moore • Gregory L. Norris • Adrienne J. Odasso • Cat Rambo • Andrew Penn Romine • David Tallerman • Tais Teng Richard Thomas • Fran Wilde • A. C. Wise • Christie Yant

Edited by Mark Teppo.

Available at independent bookstores everywhere.

http://www.underlandpress.com

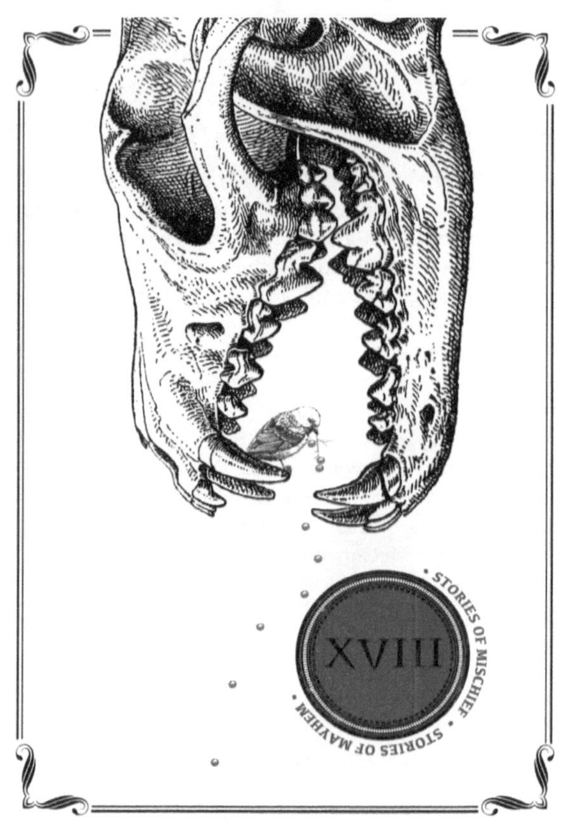

XVIII
STORIES OF MISCHIEF
STORIES OF MAYHEM

XVIII

The eighteenth Tarot card is the Moon, and those who raise their arms to her know she offers Mercy and Severity in equal measure. This is the great river at night, where wolves howl and all doors are open. All futures are possible, and every truth is elusive. This is the source and passion of *Eighteen: Stories of Mischief & Mayhem*. These twenty-four stories from voices—old and new—celebrate the inevitability of fate, the horror of prophecy, and the shivering delight of not knowing what comes next.

Cross over the threshold with us, and explore the strange, the weird, and the fantastic. Do not fear what lies ahead. It is the same as what came before. The only difference is you. This is *Eighteen*, and nothing will be the same.

With stories by Forrest Aguirre • Darin Bradley • Christopher East • Scott Edelman • Nicole Feldringer • Ben Gamblin • Ingrid Garcia • A. P. Howell • Emma Johnson-Rivard • E. E. King • Jessie Kwak • Shannon Lawrence • Gerri Leen • Mark Mills • Christi Nogle Tammie Painter • Josh Rountree • Erica Sage • Lorraine Schein • J. Dee Stanley • Richard Thomas • John Waterfall • Wendy N. Wagner • Todd Zack

Edited by Mark Teppo.

Available at independent bookstores everywhere.

www.ingramcontent.com/pod-product-compliance
Lightning Source LLC
Chambersburg PA
CBHW050416110726